I0769981

No part of this publication may be reproduced, stored in a retrieval system, or transmitted in any form or by any means, electronic, mechanical, photocopying, recording, scanning, or otherwise, without the prior written permission of the publisher, except in the case of brief quotations within critical reviews and otherwise as permitted by copyright law.

NOTE: This is a work of fiction. Names, characters, places, and incidents are a product of the author's imagination. Any resemblance to real life is purely coincidental. All characters in this story are 18 or older.

Ronan
&
Brooklyn

Willow Winters &
M. Robinson

From USA Today bestselling authors, Willow Winters and M. Robinson, comes a flirty forbidden romance.

Expensive.
Powerful.
And entirely f*cked up.

That sums up the pretentious - but elite - circle I grew up in. As much as I hate it, this life has its perks. If I want it, it's mine. It's as simple as that.
Until she showed up; she's a tempting little vixen I'm not allowed to have.

One intense night changed it all between us, threatening to shatter everything we know.

She came up with a lie. I came up with a cover. Because the truth is...

I can't keep my hands off her and one night would never be enough.

COME
HERE AND
KISS ME

PROLOGUE

RONAN

I brush the glass edge of the whiskey bottle against her swollen nub. She writhes and softly moans on the bartop as much as she can.

The silk ties around her wrists don't allow much movement. She still tries to make herself comfortable, fully aware that her heady movements aren't doing much for her current disposition. She isn't going anywhere unless I want her to.

She's at my mercy.

Mine.

She's bound to the draft pours with another tie blindfolding her beautiful, bright hazel eyes. The light freckles on her nose only entice my desire to run my tongue over them as her perky breasts are flush against my bare chest. Those gorgeous legs of hers are spread so her ass sits on the edge, right on my hard, throbbing cock, while her red-bottomed heels perch on the bar.

I take another swig of the bottle and wipe my mouth with the back of my hand. She tastes of expensive sin that could cost me everything all at once. Yet I can't stop myself.

I can't stop this.

What's happening between us is like nothing I've ever experienced.

For a second, I roughly grip her slender waist, and she purrs in response to my frenzied assault. I can't get enough of her. This little minx obviously likes it rough, and I have no fucking problem showing her a side of me she's never seen before.

Brooklyn's dirty-blond hair tosses carelessly as I suck her nipple into my mouth. I fucking want to see those plump, pouty lips part again for me and only me. Give me those little moans and strangled sighs of pleasure as the ecstasy I deliver makes her melt against my touch.

Light filters through the bar, highlighting the rows of colored glass and dark amber woods. A car drives past us, and my heart races at the thought of someone seeing us in this sinful predicament. Looking over my shoulder, I check once more that the blinds are closed. No one should be here since the bar closed over an hour ago.

Despite that, I still risked it all by having her pussy spread wide open for me. Even knowing that, it still doesn't stop what happened next between us. If anything, it only adds to the heightened emotions lingering in the air and wreaking havoc on our minds as I continue to cross the line from her being my enemy to now my lover.

The thought prompts me to take another swig. I drip the whiskey from my mouth onto her clit and to the opening of her cunt, then take a slow, torturous lick. Sliding two fingers into her warm, welcoming heat, I curve them and finger fuck her until her thighs shake and hips buck, and she's seconds from calling out my name.

"Stay fucking still and take what I give you, my little whore," I murmur as I press the weight of my body against hers to keep her pinned against the bar. She obeys like the good girl she is for me.

Ever since I first laid eyes on her, I've wanted to fuck her until she screams my name and surrenders to me. My zipper fills the deafening silence, and I let my suit pants pool to the floor beneath me. She swallows, the cords in her throat tightening, and the blush in her chest creeps up her sleek neck to her high, prominent cheekbones and then her temples. I'm silent as I watch her, knowing if we do this, there's no fucking way anyone can know.

She may think she's rebelling from her rich prick of a father by having a sordid night and forbidden affair with a professor at her father's university. Her old man is the dean, so he can never find out.

And it can never happen again...

From the stolen glances that last far too long to the way her lips tilt up when she says my name, it's as if she's teasing and taunting me all at the same time. Every little touch she's tempted me with over the years that no one else sees can never happen again.

Not after what we did tonight.

"Ro." She moans my name as her body trembles with pleasure. Her back arches slightly, and her hair turns into a messy halo on the bartop as her head falls back with those sweet sounds uttered from her swollen lips.

With the last of the whiskey, I toss back half, then savor the other half, staring down at her gorgeous body laid bare in front of me. Swishing the expensive liquor once, I hover over her, nudging her nose with mine, and let the whiskey fall to her lips. She's such a good fucking girl, taking what I offer her. Our lips meet, and I kiss her with the desire and torment that's built up over the years.

The bottle slams to the table as I lose myself in her kiss.

In her body.

In the sin of it all.

Us.

One hand on her hip keeps her where I need her while the other strokes my cock, and I line myself up to her wet cunt.

In one hard thrust, I'm deep inside her, taking everything I've always wanted and knew I couldn't have.

I'm reckless as I fuck her senseless.

She didn't come here for me tonight.

None of this should have ever happened.

But I'll be damned if I don't give in to the temptation that is this woman. Especially when it's presented so easily, so willingly... a fucking gorgeous enticement.

A precious gift.

A heated moment.

One night of doing the very thing we know we shouldn't.

I try not to think about the consequences of my actions. I try not to let myself think about the future. Instead, I lose myself inside her.

Panting.

Sweating.

Moaning.

Coming...

Loud.

Hard.

"Ro!" she screams in ecstasy, squeezing the fuck out of my cock.

I thought last night would be our first and last time—

until this morning when I got an email and a video proving someone else saw everything. I don't know who was watching or how the hell it happened. But as I press the play button on the anonymous email, I know damn well someone saw and knew exactly what they would do with the recording of us.

"Fuck!"

CHAPTER 1

BROOKLYN

I'm too fucking tired for this.

The incessant vibrating of my phone is at war with my pounding headache, which is likely a hangover. Holding in a groan, I attempt to get out of bed, but I miss the warmth of the luxurious sheets and fluffy comforter instantly as I reach for my damn phone.

Buzz, buzz.

My phone vibrates as my eyes adjust to the early morning light. What time is it? Clicking the side button on my cell, I read 6:42 a.m. The messages from my father's texts are in all caps.

"Shit," I murmur. Tossing the phone back onto the nightstand, I hit the modern crystal lamp that cost a fortune.

Fuck being up this early, and fuck those texts. Whatever my overbearing and demanding father wants can wait. The sheets call to me, but I toss and turn with my pounding headache. I'm overly anxious, knowing I have angry texts waiting for me when I get up. Unable to fall back asleep, I fling the sheets off my body, dead set on dealing with today once a few painkillers have a chance to kick in.

Slipping on my silk-bowed pink slippers, I make my way to the bathroom in my loft apartment on Fifth Avenue and toss back the pills. With its artsy abstract cut, the gold-rimmed mirror holds an object that makes me cringe. My deep burgundy silk strap nightgown hangs from my left shoulder, and my dirty-blond hair is a halo of a mess. My mascara is smeared, and my lips are stained from the wine last night.

My thighs clench at the memory of him, and even with all the bullshit I've been dealing with recently, I have to bite down on a smile.

Last night.

Ronan.

How the hell did I not wake up immediately thinking of him and how scandalously sweet our rendezvous was?

My reminiscing is cut short with the banging on my front door. At first, I fear it's my father. But somehow, my heart sinks even lower when I hear Ronan call out my name.

In a rather pissed-off tone, he snarls, "Brooklyn!"

My heart sinks, and my head spins as I try to remember

exactly how last night ended. With confusion and uncertainty escorting me, I cautiously make my way to the front door.

"Brooklyn, open the damn door!" he orders in a scolding tone, and I'm instantly pissed.

He's not my fucking father, even if he is older than me and I enjoyed him bossing me around last night. That was last night when passion overruled my reasoning. I grip the lock and slide it over so hard that it doesn't pop out.

The second the struggle is over, I whip the door open and demand, "The fuck is your problem?"

I don't bother to hold back my anger, even if my heart beats as if it's trying to bust through the cage that holds it inside me.

You and me both, buddy.

I leave the door open, with Ronan standing there, narrowed eyes with a devilish spark and consuming composure.

"What was so damn important that you had to wake me up?" I lie, blaming him because, really, if he's mad at me, I want him to know I'm mad at him too.

Anxiousness slips through me as I cross my arms and sink into the deep navy velvet sofa. It sits perpendicular to the floor-to-ceiling windows that showcase the hustle and bustle of New York shops below and the breathtaking sight of the skyline above. Ronan stares a moment longer, his gaze boring into me, and I stare back just as intently. It takes him a second to step inside and close the door behind him. All the while, it's silent as if he's judging me, and all I can think is … what the hell happened last night?

I thought it was mutual. I thought he enjoyed himself as much as I did. What the hell did I do? Tears threaten to prick at the back of my eyes, so I bury those emotions deep, deep down inside me where they belong. I've had a crush on this man since I was far too young, and he was far too old for me. I won't be made to feel ashamed of last night by anyone.

Including him.

Especially him.

"You didn't answer your phone," he says in a sedated tone but still tight in accusation.

"My father is being … well … my father, so I'm ignoring it." I pick at my nails as he takes a cautious step forward.

A sharp pain at my temple reminds me of my predicament, so rather than waiting for whatever the hell he has to say, I get up and make my way to the kitchen.

"I need coffee," I tell him as a means of an explanation, and he follows.

It's then that it hits me. He's never been in my apartment. Suddenly, my cheeks heat with the realization. The kitchen is smaller than I'd like, but it's not like I cook anyway. I pop a pod into the coffee maker and hit the button, then quickly remember to slip a mug into place.

"What do you want?" I ask, turning around to lean the small of my back against the counter. "If it's to thank me for last night, you're very welcome," I sass with my asymmetrical smile remaining tight as he doesn't respond with a better mood.

At least he has the decency to avert his eyes.

As he swallows thickly, my gaze focuses on the cords tightening his neck and the five o'clock shadow around his sharp jaw. My brow furrows when I realize he's wearing the same shirt and pants from last night. Or at least I think he is. The white tee is slightly wrinkled, like he slept in it, though it's still tight on his broad shoulders. His suit pants are like any other black suit pants, so I suppose maybe it's not the same.

However, I choose to think it's the latter.

The worst yet best part is that he smells like last night—of sex and sin and that intoxicating cologne he always wears. And his hair, hell, I might as well have just fisted it as he devoured me. It's a messy sight, mirroring me.

It's quiet for a minute as I wait for him to say something. Anything.

I motion for some response.

"New place?" he questions, looking around while my gaze drops for only a moment before finding his eyes again. This time, he's staring right at me.

"It's just my parents' old place. I'm staying here for now," I reply, tending back to my coffee as the sputtering of the machine comes to an end. I don't tell him about the argument with my father or how he forced me to go to his university.

After stirring a touch of cream and sugar into my coffee, I

add, "I'll be here while I go to your school."

"Right, about that," he remarks as he stands on the kitchen threshold.

My pulse quickens. I swear to God, if he tells me I need to drop out, I think I'll throw this mug at him. I don't even want to be at their university. I have to go or else my father will... Well, he'll threaten to cut me off and order me to do something else I don't want to. It's the way it's always been. Either I march in line with his strict rules or I'm out on my ass with no money or trust fund. I won't survive. Much to my disappointment, all I know is my father's money.

I take in a steadying breath. "What about it?"

"Have you gotten an email or a message from anyone?" he asks out of nowhere, once again with a cautious tone.

I confidently state, "I've seen your dick. You've been inside me. So why are you talking to me like I'm suddenly under investigation?"

"Then you're saying it wasn't you?"

Nearly slamming my mug down on the marble counter, I can't help the exasperation as I respond, "What wasn't me?"

"Check your email," he tells me. I pick up my coffee and walk with purpose right by him, letting my side brush against his when he doesn't get out of my way in time.

I ignore him and try not to listen to his footsteps as I go back to my bedroom, the thick curtains keeping it shadowed compared to the living room. I scroll past the texts from my father, past the missed calls from both him and Ronan, and check my email. My heart races and my stomach drops, though I don't know what I'm waiting for.

"There's nothing here," I call out, then turn around to have a damn heart attack. Unbeknownst to me, Ronan stands at the foot of my bed, catching me by surprise. I wasn't aware he was that close to me, and it's both a blessing and a curse.

"Jesus fuck," I gasp with the hand holding my phone over my heart.

"Sorry," he softly utters. "I didn't mean to scare you. I'm just … fuck."

"What?" I insist, sitting on the edge of my bed.

Ronan paces with his head back and his hands in his hair.

Shaking my head, I'm still confused by the turn of events. "What is wrong with you?"

"They know!" he shouts, abruptly turning to face me.

I've never seen him like this. I've only ever known this powerful man to be controlled, calm, and composed. It both thrills me and frightens me that he's showing me a side of him I didn't know existed. Ronan is older, and his family is slightly wealthier than mine, but there's a darkness about him that fills the air around him to bend to his will. He's always gotten everything he's wanted and been out of reach.

For me.

And for everyone.

CHAPTER 2

BROOKLYN

I don't know what to do with the man standing before me. There's so much I want to say, yet I can't fathom one single thought of what he's talking about or why he's in my place to begin with.

I think back on his earlier question. "How did you know where I was staying?"

He's again at the foot of my bed, indignant over something he seems to blame me for. He swallows so hard this time, I hear it before he looks me dead in the eyes.

In one determined breath, he informs me, "There's a video of us last night."

My heart sinks, and my blood goes cold as my unsteady

stare widens.

"You're lying," I spew without knowing if there's even a real possibility that this could indeed happen.

"It was emailed to me, and the university board was cc'd."

I lightly gasp, taking in his words as if he just told me hell has frozen over, and in a way, it has.

What. The. Fuck.

In seconds, his eyes shine with rage and disbelief and regret. Making me feel like shit and ashamed.

"The board?" I repeat in disbelief, almost like I need to hear myself say it out loud to him.

That's when it becomes real.

A nightmare come to life.

I open my mouth to ask about my father, but he reads my mind and cuts me off. "Yes, your father was cc'd as well."

I stumble back, unable to hold myself upright for a second.

"Don't look at me like that," he orders in a stern voice, cocking his head to the side.

"Like what?"

"Like this is my fault."

I resist the urge to attack him. Instead, I snap, "Who the fuck videoed us and emailed them?" My entire body shakes with anger, embarrassment, and even fear. Fear of what is to come...

From my father.

The university.

Ronan?

"It was anonymous, but they called for my resignation."

My bottom lip drops open as I realize what he's saying. Ronan's a professor, but he doesn't have tenure yet. They'll fire him for this. My father, the dean, will make sure of it. No one crosses him.

Ever.

"What the fuck?" That's all I can manage to whisper. "That explains the texts from my father."

"Give it." He snatches my cell phone out of my hand.

Fuck me.

I fall back onto the bed, the sheets unfortunately cold now, and blink away all thoughts of my father. I try to focus on last night and the reality that a video of what happened between us got out. My throat goes dry. It's not like I have a stellar reputation, but I don't need any more judgment. I don't want people to see me at my most vulnerable.

Naked.

Spread eagle.

Begging to make me come.

It's hard to breathe as Ronan drones on, cussing at something my father sent. I'm there, but I'm not. It's like I'm having an out-of-body experience, hanging on for dear life.

"Are you even listening to me?"

Feeling snarky, I remind him, "I thought I did a great job of listening to you last night. I was such a good girl for you, remember?"

"I'm serious, Brooklyn."

Not backing down, I insist, "So am I."

Something about his tone begs me to look back at him. He tosses my phone on my bed and swallows hard. His Adam's apple is prominent in his throat, catching my attention without even trying. Heat overwhelms me, recalling the way my lips felt against his skin. Even if he is a selfish prick, Ronan has always done something to me that no one else ever has.

I thought last night would be a release. Just a one-night escape from the shit happening in my life. From everything I've been running away from, landing right in his arms and on his dick. Panic threatens to overwhelm me, but I don't show him. I remain stoic and unbothered. That's my reputation, and I have no plans of letting him see the real me.

Nobody does.

Not even my family.

I'm just a rich bitch who can't get anything right. If they show that video, it'll only harden my armor. It has to. The other option is to wither away to the nothingness my father tells me I am.

"You don't care that I could lose my fucking job, do you?"

His accusation throws me in a tailspin. "Don't take your bullshit out on me," I scold, abruptly standing in his face.

Men like Ronan need to be put in their place, and I have no problem being the woman to do that.

"You knew who you were fucking."

"I never thought it'd get out."

Pretending that doesn't hurt me, I add, "I guess I couldn't be your dirty little secret, Professor Wolf."

Again, he swallows thickly.

"But to answer your question, of course I care," I stress, attempting to think straight.

He closes the distance between us. Close enough for the heat from his body to add to the tension in mine. For the first time since I unlocked my front door, he looks at me as if he's actually seeing me. My heart beats wildly as his thumb falls to my bottom lip, and I'm left helpless. I hate what this man does to me. I make a pitiful attempt not to melt into his simple but pungent touch.

"If you want me to touch you again, you'll mind the way you speak to me," he warns with fire in his eyes that causes my thighs to clench.

It takes everything in me to answer. "Is that a threat, Professor Wolf?"

His lips lift in an asymmetrical way. A cocky, arrogant ... yet something else. Something desirable that only he possesses.

With a wicked grin, he coaxes, "Only if you want it to be."

In the blink of an eye, I'm reminded of last night.

The liberation.

The release.

His scent.

His touch.

It's overpowering.

He's older, thirty-five, and I'm only twenty-two. He's a professor, and I'm a student who only got accepted because my father's the dean and made it happen.

And our families... enemies isn't quite the right word. Enemies stab you in the front. Our families aim for the back while smiling to your face. That's how these circles run and always have since I was a little girl, simply surviving this bullshit. I'm as much of a victim as he is in this unexpected situation we've found ourselves in.

I thought I'd get over the temptation that Ronan is, but I want nothing more than to have him again.

He makes me forget.

He makes me feel free.

Desired.

Wanted.

Needed.

Loved?

Again, I'm unable to resist his control over me, and I reach up to kiss him, but it's short-lived. He pulls back slightly, and I miss him instantly. Thankfully, he drops his lips for another kiss, and it's just as hot and electric as the first.

"You're nothing but the forbidden fruit I want to fuck," he whispers against my lips.

I open them slowly and wait for his to open before responding. "And you're nothing but a mistake I can't get enough of."

There's a moment between us, unspoken and raw, or maybe it's simply in my fucked-up head and a delusion I've made up about us. But an idea comes to me. To piss them all off and maybe to save myself and him in the process.

"I have an idea," I proclaim, and he straightens.

"What's that?"

"It's self-serving, but it's the only way you can keep your job."

"I'm a professor, and you're a student. No amount of money can be thrown at your old man or the board to keep my job."

"Trust me, it's not money. I have an idea. Just trust me," I adamantly repeat as I push the hair out of my face and ready myself for what has to happen.

His brow arches. "Since when are you trustworthy?" he questions, and it hurts more than I wish it did.

"Since I decided I like what you do to me."

A heat simmers between us as our eyes lock, and I hold on to that.

I hold on to him.

He licks his lower lip. "Tell me how we could possibly fix this?"

I don't hesitate to respond with a smile before I tell him the plan to save both our asses from the wrath of my father.

The dean.

His boss.

CHAPTER 3

RONAN

The room smells of leather, as it always has since I was a young man. The polished walnut table and carved wingback chairs have sat here on the sixth floor of the university for decades. The large paned windows overlook the lush green campus, and for the longest time, this has been my sanctuary, my fucking dream.

However, today, it's my literal hell.

Not everyone is here, and I'm thankful for that. Full attendance of the board is a rarity and certainly for emergency meetings. Men I've looked up to for years, men who served as my professors when I went here, stare back at me in crisp suits and expensive silk ties, their eyes judging and full of disappointment or disgust. It's hard to gauge.

I'll admit the video wasn't the most moral of engagements.

I fucked Brooklyn without mercy and enjoyed every second of it with every sinful fantasy I've ever had of her, and there's no fucking way I can deny that. It's obvious in the video. My lust for her spills in the 4k resolution.

I clear my throat, and the room stills with a deafening silence. They're simply waiting for me to speak as I stand at the head of the table. The only movement comes from the swaying of a chair at the other end. The light from the windows casts a shadow down Brooklyn's father's considerable frame. His narrowed eyes nearly match the black of his suit.

I stare directly at them as I announce, "I'm aware that this meeting is due to the email sent this morning."

"Professor Wolf," Mr. Micheals declares, a man I've respected for as long as I can remember. Dominick Michaels has been an adviser at the university since before I was born. The old man was a mentor to me when I first applied.

I turn to him, heat gripping the back of my neck. I've known him for nearly two decades. The last thing I want is the expression of regret on his face and his tone of condolences.

"You understand why we have to do this, I'm sure," he comments, and I shake my head in denial. His role at the university is the provost, and he's never preferred the title Professor over the mundane. Mr. Michaels has seniority, so if I can win him over, there's a chance in hell we can survive this.

"Unfortunately, the email and video sent are out of my control, but it's not on the board to take action," I state, and the lies at the back of my throat nearly make my voice tight. Nearly, but somehow I'm able to be firm in my response.

Mr. Michaels flinches back, surprised by my statement.

"I had no idea that I was being recorded in the private establishment I own."

"Not just you." The hard tone from Dean Chambers, Brooklyn's father, is met with the slamming of his fist at the end of the table. "You weren't the only one recorded," he reaffirms with a menacing tone.

Quite honestly, I can't blame the prick for his barely contained anger. After all, what I did to his daughter last night is something I'm sure no father would ever want to see. Especially his little girl.

"No, it wasn't just me. You see..." I pause for a second, catching my bearings before I drop what can only be described as the biggest lie of my life. Standing my ground, I confess with more ease than I thought possible. "My fiancée was also filmed last night without her consent."

Adrenaline soars through my veins as several men loudly gasp, and the lone woman on the board stares back at me with wide eyes of disbelief as she repeats, "Your fiancée?"

"Yes, of course. That's the only reason I'd ever engage in that manner with a university student. I'm sure you can understand that she and I—"

"Bullshit!" her father roars at the end of the table. Huffing and puffing like a fucking lunatic. As his chest rises and falls, it dawns on him that the room is calm, that this is a far better resolution for the board and the university than filing anything or making any statements to the public.

With all eyes on him, he readjusts his tie and sits back, not daring to look at anyone else.

"Yes." I spin back to Mrs. Sanders. "As you can imagine, my fiancée is mortified, as am I, that we were taken advantage of and that someone would violate our intimate privacy in that manner."

I can barely breathe, my entire body on fire as I wait to see if it works. If they believe me. If they'll allow this to slide and let it be. It's truly best for all of them except for the one man at the end of the table, parallel to me, who's probably contemplating my murder. If it weren't for any witnesses, he more than likely would. I try not to relish in the feeling of knowing he hates me just as much as I hate him, and now I'm engaged to his only daughter.

In the end, I win.

"The board will do everything in our power to help identify this individual." Mr. Michaels speaks up, breaking the tension in the room.

I remember the look on Brooklyn's face this morning and the anger at whoever the fuck dared take advantage of her. With that thought in mind, I thank Mr. Michaels. She doesn't deserve that shit.

I run a hand through my hair and thank the board for their discretion and understanding. All the while, glimpses of Brooklyn from that video and from real life last night as she writhed under me flash before my eyes.

Fuck.

My cock hardens at the thought.

It's an odd sensation that comes over me... The desire to fucking murder whoever saw Brooklyn with me and recorded us while being grateful for not losing my job and the last decade of my career just barely being saved by this lie she planned for us.

"Congratulations on your engagement," Mrs. Sanders says while standing. "I don't believe there's anything else to discuss at this time." She's quick to leave, no doubt unimpressed with the entire ordeal.

The room empties out, and I'm uncertain if they believe we're engaged or if they're just relieved they don't have to deal with the scandal. Either way, half don't look me in the eyes as they leave. They all look at Dean Chambers, though, but he doesn't bother to spare them a glance. He stays seated, his chair swaying slowly left and right, and I wait just like he does for everyone else to leave.

I'm fully aware this isn't the end of our conversation. If anything, it's just the beginning.

My collar is hot and tight at my neck as I stare down

Brooklyn's father. My cufflinks are buffed and shine with wealth. I've known this man all my life—from poker nights with my father and social gatherings and galas. From contracts and business deals gone wrong, we wrecked any professional relationship we might have had.

He's never looked at me with so much disdain. Even after all the shit we've been through, never like this. Hell I probably know him better than my father, his former friend and longtime foe, does. Both of our families have fuck you money most can't even comprehend… but fucking his daughter? Hell, even a prick like me knows better.

I know how money moves and how much is at stake. So I patiently wait, biding my time. All the while, the memory of Brooklyn's cunt and how good she felt keeps me wondering if last night was worth it.

"Does your father know about this?" he questions when we're left with nothing but tormenting silence. The door to the conference room remains open, so he keeps his voice low. Not wanting anyone to hear what he has to say to me.

I clear my throat. "I've yet to tell him." I hold his gaze, and all I see is spite from a man who has every right to hate me.

"And what do you think he'll have to say about—"

"She's my fiancée," I stress as if that's going to smooth over the ripples it'll cause in social circles that fucking matter.

"Bullshit," her father practically spits. He holds nothing but venom as he spews, "There's no fucking way she'd ever be with a man like you."

My lips pick up into a smirk at a thought.

She said something about daddy issues...

I keep the remark to myself. Not because I don't want to piss him off, but more because I wouldn't put it past him to record the conversation to fuck me over with it. The Chambers can't be trusted, and now I'm supposedly engaged to one.

I clench my jaw at the thought. For years, I've wanted her, and the one night I fall prey to her charm, it's fucking recorded. There's no chance this is a coincidence.

Without a response, he gets back to the issue at hand, wanting to destroy my life and get me fired. "You fucked a student, and you won't—"

"I fucked my future wife," I interject, wanting the upper hand. Tension rises in my shoulders.

"There are forms and protocols when relationships..." He starts as if he's found a loophole.

"I have yet to send them, but I have time," I inform him. I'm certain the forms need to be filed within months. She's just transferred, and the semester starts next week. "I have time," I repeat.

"This is a crock of shit, and you and I both know it," he bites out, his patience wearing thin. There's also a hint of defeat in his tone.

"I believe we all have a vested interest in our private

lives staying private," I tell him with an arched eyebrow and determined stance.

"Who sent the video?"

"I don't know."

"Who took it?" he questions, anger rolling through his shoulders.

"I don't know."

"You fucking did it, you lying prick," he accuses.

I bite my tongue, knowing I'm the one whose career will end if anything happens. My shoulders are tight, my muscles coiled as I inform him that I will let him know once I discover who violated my privacy.

I nearly say "who violated your daughter," but again, I bite my tongue for the sake of my tenure.

"Do I need to remind you that I'm a professor of law at your university? My lawyers are already on it. I took care of that this morning." There will be multiple meetings, and lawyers talking to lawyers. It could be months, but I will find out. I'll know, and they'll fucking pay. Only then can this facade of matrimony be laid to rest.

"When exactly did the two of you decide to get married?" he continues the interrogation.

"Last week," I spit the lie out quickly.

"What are the odds that your story and my daughter's story will match?"

"What are the odds that she's talking to you?" I retort,

pushing back for the first time.

"She will... if she wants her trust fund. Unless she no longer needs it. I assume since the two of you are getting married. Fifty-fifty?" he goads.

I think about telling him just how well I've done at taking care of his daughter, but a flash of someone's suit walking by the open door brings me back to the present moment.

"We discussed a prenup ... specifically not having one. Although none of this is the concern of the board or to you."

He rises, and I half expect him to flip the damn table, but instead, he adjusts his tie and keeps his voice even as he threatens me, "Keep your fucking hands off my daughter, or I'll destroy you. Your family. Your name will be a curse in every business and academic circle." The sharpness of his blue eyes and the disgust that coats his tone are ones I'm familiar with.

All the fucked-up responses rebound in the back of my mind. I think about telling him how it's her hands that were all over me, and that's why I tied them up.

Instead, I offer him a pressed smile. "Have a good week, Dean Chambers."

I walk to the door with only thoughts of Brooklyn's gorgeous body and what I plan to do with it in my mind. "I know I will."

With that, I exit the room with my lie fueling the fire of what is still to come between us all.

CHAPTER 4

BROOKLYN

All day yesterday, I avoided my father like the fucking plague until I can't

anymore. I have to leave soon to meet him, but I don't want to move from the corner seat in the living room. It's my depression spot, sunken cushion and all. The clock ticks, and I realize I spent most of the morning trying to figure out what I would say to him. And I've come up with nothing.

As my freshly polished nails tap on the empty crystal glass, I don't know where to start. I never do with my father. I've spent most of my life feeling like he resents me because my mother cheated on him and left him for another man.

She cheated on that one too and moved overseas, so I

suppose it's a consolation prize for him.

I guess it doesn't matter that she left both of us, saying she has a new chance at life. I rarely see her, and when I do, it never ends well. From the moment they divorced, my father became a different man. There are days when I don't recognize him, and sometimes I feel like he knows it.

I mean, how many times do you have to remind someone they aren't good enough for them to believe it? It's all he ever tells me, and at some point, it becomes good enough to know you'll never be good enough.

I shake the thought out of my mind and shift my attention to the text message that dings on my phone. Thinking it's my father, I grab it and realize it's my best friend, Aspen, instead. Her ding is followed by a string of other messages from the group chat we're in with our close friends. My gut sinks, and I have to shove down the anxiousness. We all grew up together. Some say we are only friends because of our family's wealth. Others say we genuinely look out for each other.

Either way, Aspen and I are like sisters. Both of us come from fucked-up families where all that matters is the bottom dollar and whether you're wearing designer clothes and live in million-dollar estates. We have a lot in common, except Aspen has her mother in her life.

We both know the pressure to be perfect on the outside while dying on the inside. It's the norm for the socialites who live on the Upper East Side of New York City. Where dreams are made with deals with the devil.

Money.

Everything and anyone has a price, and I learned that at a very early age. Aspen and I both have. Our family's drama gives soap operas a run for their money. I can't make up the shit my father has done to stay the wealthiest and sway politicians and brokers. Now he runs the most prestigious university, putting him at the top of the hierarchy. Exactly where he thinks he belongs.

I like to think of it more as a food chain and every person for themselves.

My cell phone begins to ding again, tearing my eyes back to the text message from Aspen.

Aspen: *Oh my God. When were you going to tell me?*

My heart drops, but I quickly compose myself and text her back.

Brooklyn: *Tell you what?*
Aspen: *Brooklyn... we all know. There's a freaking video!*
Brooklyn: *Know what?*

My whole life comes crashing down the second she texts...

Aspen: *We saw the video.*

I gasp, jerking back. How the fuck did they get it? Who the fuck told them? No.... no... Fucking no! The force of her words literally makes my body shudder as if a gush of wind just knocked the shit out of me. It doesn't take me long to put two and two together.

They know.

Aspen: *Are you going to say something?????*

I don't reply, frozen where I stand, tightly gripping my phone. Fuck!

Brooklyn: *Who sent you the video?*
Aspen: *That's what you reply?*
Brooklyn: *I'll explain everything. Just tell me who sent it to you.*
Aspen: *It was emailed anonymously to all of us. Does your dad know?*
Brooklyn: *Unfortunately.*
Aspen: *About the video or your history with him?*

Seeing that question written out for me, clear as day, throws me for a loop and yanks me right back to that place and time when Ronan had just become Professor Wolf...

A time before I knew how fucked this life was. A time I wouldn't dare disobey my father.

6 YEARS AGO

"I can't believe your dad is now the dean," Christoff announces to our friends.

Six of us sit around the clothed table in the middle of the hall—three guys and three girls.

"I can." I sigh, sitting back in the seat. My eyes never leave my father, who shakes hands with every man in a polished suit in the room. "It's always been his number one priority. Running the university means he thinks he runs everything now."

Christoff knowingly remarks, "You'll have to play nice now, Brooklyn. Being the dean's daughter comes with a lot of pressure."

I scoff out a chuckle. "You mean getting drunk at this gala is out of the question?" I grab the pink flask filled with expensive tequila out of my purse, compliments of my father's well-stocked wine and liquor cellar. He's oblivious to what he has in there, so he'll never notice anything is gone. I gulp a big swig before offering it to Christoff, who shakes his head.

William grabs it from me with a wicked smile and nods.

Our group of friends are what you call the crème de la crème. Everyone wants to be us or be seen with us, and we don't accept new people into our clique unless you bring something to the table. And by that, I mean knowledge is always power.

I take another gulp and put the flask back in my purse before I make my way inside the extravagant building hosting this charity event. I may not be able to legally drink, but I'm still seventeen and practically an adult. As soon as I walk into the banquet hall, I see him standing at the bar.

Professor Wolf.

My heart does that weird thing I hate. My body is numb, and I stand staring for far too long.

He's surrounded by beautiful women. He always is. Quite the ladies' man, from what I hear. People love to gossip, and when you look as good as he does, you give a lot of people reasons to talk about you. I've known him since I was a little girl, but he never pays me any mind. He doesn't even know I exist because he's too busy working his way to the top.

I watch him as he effortlessly flirts and gives each of the women the attention they crave.

He always has this presence about him without even trying. When he walks into a room, people stop and listen. My father has the same effect.

A sense of jealousy washes over me for no reason whatsoever. Not once in the past ten years when I've seen him from afar at galas, functions, parties, etc. has the man acknowledged my existence. The list of how many times we've been in the same room together is endless.

Swallowing hard, I roll my eyes and exit the room onto the balcony. Alone at last. At times, I long for it. Being in a room full of people, feeling like you're screaming but no one is listening. It happens to me at least once a day. I'm used to it by now.

I hear footsteps behind me before Christoff's voice fills the air between us.

"There you are."

I don't bother to turn around. "You're looking for me?"

He lightly chuckles. "I like your dress."

My friendship with Christoff has always been flirtatious. It's just how we are with one another. If I'm the pack leader, then he's right behind me with his blond hair and bright blue eyes. He reminds me of a rougher version of the perfect prince.

Within seconds, he cages me in from behind with his muscular, fit arms.

"I'm more curious about what's under your dress..."

I giggle, but before I can spin to face him, a rough voice echoes around us. "Your father is looking for you, Christoff."

I snap around, recognizing Professor Wolf.

Christoff meets his neutral stare, retorting, "And he sent you to fetch me?"

"I wouldn't keep him waiting, boy," Professor Wolf emphasizes the last word, and I arch an eyebrow.

After Christoff leaves, Professor Wolf adds, "You should stay away from him. That kid is nothing but bad news."

This is the first time Ronan has said anything to me, and I try to act as if it doesn't faze me when it most definitely does. Luckily, I've been playing different roles my entire life, and this moment is no exception.

I shrug. "He's one of my closest friends."

"You know what they say. You are the company you keep."

Unable to hold back, I curiously ask, "What's it to you? You're suddenly my keeper?"

"I suggest you find new friends, Brooklyn."

Surprised, I blurt, "You know my name?"

"Doesn't everyone? You're the dean's little girl."

Feeling brazen, I seductively lean against the railing. "Does it look like I'm a little girl?"

He eyes me up and down for a moment, and I swear my heart drums faster against my chest.

Ignoring my question, he backs away, coaxing, "Don't say I didn't warn you."

With that, he turns and leaves. I'm about to step off the balcony when I see my father glaring daggers at the new professor out of the corner of my eye. It's only then I realize Daddy doesn't like him, and I can't help but love that.

CHAPTER 5

BROOKLYN

A text from my father brings me back to the present, and I'm reminded that I'm supposed to leave soon to have lunch with him. Fucking hell.

Dad: *You get to be what you always wanted—a trophy wife, just like your mother.*

His text hurts in the same way he knows it will. My father is never one to beat around the bush, especially regarding how he treats and speaks to me. I answer Aspen.

Brooklyn: *I'll call you later and fill you in.*

Aspen: *You promise?*

Brooklyn: *Cross my heart.*

Almost immediately, I receive another text message from Ronan. I've been ignoring him too.

Ronan: *Where are you?*

His text pisses me off as much as my father's. I'd be lying if I said it doesn't make me want to call the whole thing off. A part of me wants to get back at him for making me attend his university. I know this is the best revenge, but another part of me doesn't want to hurt him.

How fucked up is that?

If that doesn't define our toxic relationship, I don't know what does. People say I'm just a spoiled little rich girl, and it's hard to defend when my dad still pulls the strings in my life. I'm dependent on him, and he never stops using it to his advantage.

In order to avoid my dad, I'm hiding out at a lavish hotel downtown. I use cash to pay for my suite so he can't find me.

So nobody can find me.

Including Professor Wolf.

Ronan: *You can't ignore me forever. You're my fiancée.*

On autopilot, I write...

Brooklyn: *Fake fiancée.*

Ronan: *It doesn't change the fact that you're mine now, so when I text you, I expect an answer. Do I make myself clear?*

I narrow my eyes at his threat.

Brooklyn: *What are you going to do? Spank me?*

Ronan: *You'd like that too much.*

Brooklyn: *Don't flatter yourself.*

Ronan: *I wasn't the one who begged for it this weekend.*

I snarl at his statement. Given I have to lie to my father who's going to scream at me, not to mention the fact that it's going around... my emotions are running high.

Brooklyn: *Fuck off. You were practically begging too.*

Ronan: *I'd much rather fuck you. Now be my good girl and tell me where you are.*

Brooklyn: *But I'm so much better at being your bad girl, Professor Wolf.*

Ronan: *I warned you.*

My cell phone makes an unfamiliar noise when all of a sudden, it looks like there's a tracker on my fucking screen.

"What in the actual fuck?"

Brooklyn: *You put a tracker on my phone?*
Ronan: *I didn't. I paid someone else to. All they needed was your number.*

My hands shake with utter rage. All I want is some privacy to think about my life as it slowly crumbles, and every bit of it is out of my control. When I don't respond, my phone pings again.

Ronan: *You weren't at your apartment. You weren't responding. I thought the worst, so you can't be pissed. I'll be there in twenty minutes.*

"Ugh!" I toss my phone across the living room, but thankfully, it lands on the couch and doesn't shatter. Taking a deep, unsteady breath, I mentally prepare for whatever the hell is next.

RONAN

I've been in my head for the past twenty-four hours, and it doesn't help that Brooklyn has blown me off. She's the one who came up with this plan, and now she pretends I don't fucking exist. I've never wanted to spank and then fuck someone so goddamn bad. It's a fucking flood of complicated emotions. One right after the other with no end in sight.

I've always had control, but for the past forty-eight hours, I've been spiraling.

I barely slept last night, tossing and turning with my mind reeling a mile a minute. I'm waiting for the fallout—the official email—but it hasn't come yet.

All Brooklyn has to do is tell her father it's a lie. And then my entire life is fucking over.

I can't lose my chance at tenure. It's years in the making. I can't control the thought that Brooklyn may have set me up.

How do I know she's not the one behind the video being emailed to the board and her father?

I don't trust her. She's a Chambers, and they're full of lies, deception, and manipulation. Hot as fucking hell but not to be trusted.

Did I play right into her hands? Can I buy my way out of this?

None of this stops the desire to call her my little whore again. I liked it.

I liked it a lot.

More than I care to admit to myself, let alone out loud to anyone else. Once I pull into the parking garage of the hotel, I rush to her room and pound on the door. I roll my sleeves up as I wait for her to answer.

After a minute, she doesn't, and I shift where I stand, brushing off my slacks and banging my fist on the door again.

"Open the door, Brooklyn!"

She flings it open, shouting, "What?"

My heart hammers, and I fucking love it. I love the heat in her gaze, her reddened lips, and that fire in her tone.

In one quick stride, I'm in her face with my hand over her mouth. I kick the door shut behind me as I back her up against the wall, locking her in place. Like the other night, she's at my mercy. My cock hardens instantly.

In the midst of having her in my arms, I quickly scour the room and see the long, narrow hallway beside us. I'm immediately assaulted by the scent of her everywhere and all around me. For a second, I feel a little lightheaded.

With a hard edge in my tone, I warn, "Tell me again that you want to call this off?"

She whimpers a moan, both pissed and turned on. She's wearing a skimpy cream nighty that leaves very little to the imagination. I'm instantly envisioning her beneath me and moaning out my name. The silk clings to her like a second skin, and I can't help but let out a tormented groan.

The reaction she stirs out of me is new to me. I'm used to being in control, and when it comes to her, I feel as if I don't have any.

"Now, are you going to be my good girl and listen to me, or am I going to have to spank you into submission? Either way, you'll hear what I have to say." Gesturing to her, I order, "Nod your pretty little head if you understand me."

She glares at me, and it hits my already hard cock like a fucking bullet. She's the one holding the loaded gun, aiming it directly at my dick. And what does she do next? The fucking minx bites my hand.

I grip her throat this time, and her eyes widen.

"Since you can't follow simple directions, I'll have to hold you hostage until you listen to what I have to say."

She opens her mouth to reply, but I grip her throat a little harder, silencing her. Not enough to hurt, not enough to cut off her breath, just enough. Just like I did the other night. She writhes under me, and I know damn well she could fight.

"I'll make you a deal."

Her gorgeous doe eyes zero in on me.

"That got your attention?"

She reluctantly nods, surrendering to me, but I don't let her go. Mostly because I like having her at my mercy.

"I want something I think you want too."

Again, her brows furrow.

"And I need you to do this for me."

She mouths, "Why?"

I don't hesitate to respond. "I need you to be my fiancée for a believable amount of time."

Little by little, I back away from her, and her hand goes to her throat, but she keeps her eyes on me. "Why do you want this now?"

"It's none of your business."

"If I'm going to be your fake fiancée, then I'm making it my business."

I cock my head to the side, grinning. "So you agree to keep this charade going?"

"Not until you tell me why."

"I'll tell you when the time is right."

In one breath, she spews, "I don't fucking trust you."

I don't waver. "The feeling's mutual, sweetheart."

"Fuck off."

Unable to resist, I grip the back of her neck and tell her, "I already told you, my little whore, I'd much rather fuck you instead."

And with that...

I slam my mouth onto hers.

CHAPTER 6

RONAN

Something primal has come over me.

Maybe it's because someone has leaked our sex tape.

Maybe it's because I'm on the verge of losing my job, the one I worked so hard for.

Or maybe it's because she agreed to this charade of being my fiancée that I need to be inside her.

So many emotions fuel my desire to thrust balls deep inside her. I don't try to control it or understand it. It only fuels the fire brewing inside me to make her scream out my name.

This may not be the right time, but I don't give a fuck.

She said yes, and that's reason enough for me to lose myself inside her.

I need her, and that's all that matters to me.

Pressing soft kisses up her neck, I confess, "You have me questioning everything about myself, Brooklyn."

She sucks in a breath, realizing the sudden change in my demeanor.

"Do you have any idea what you're doing to me?"

She peeks up at me through her lashes, simply questioning, "How do you go from zero to a hundred?"

"You're my fiancée now. I'm just taking what belongs to me."

"Oh yeah?"

I nod, kissing her lips once again.

"Then show me."

I reach up, stroking the side of her cheek. Her face leans into my embrace. Shifting my hand to the back of her neck, I tug her closer to my mouth. Her lips find mine, and what starts off as a peck turns into something else entirely. Taking on a life of its own. I open my mouth and seek out her tongue, and it's fucking explosive. We explore each other's mouths. Our tongues twist as we taste one another. It feels amazing.

She feels amazing.

But like everything with Brooklyn, it quickly moves on its own accord. I grip onto the sides of her face, kissing her more aggressively than before. All the buildup and stress of the day has been just fucking foreplay. Having her at my mercy is better than I imagined.

My fingers move down her chest in an agonizing motion.

She holds her breath as I cup her breasts, softly kneading them while still devouring her mouth. Nothing can prepare me for this moment.

Her moaning.

Panting.

The way she rocks her hips on my hard cock.

Our legs entwine, rubbing together and moving all around. I kiss along her jawline and her neck, then deliberately make my way back up to her lips. I no longer have any control over my movements.

"Fuck ... Brook," I rumble into her mouth. I press my hand over her throat. "There's only so much restraint I have left for you."

Her eyes widen. "Yes..."

My restraint snaps.

Loud and clear.

My eyes glaze over like a possessed man as my jaw clenches. My thumb glides over her mouth before I growl, tearing at her dress.

"Hey! That's my dress!"

"I'll buy you a new one." With that, I rip it off.

Until all she's left in is her panties and bra.

"Christ, you're fucking gorgeous."

Unable to hold back, I strip her naked, leaving her bare in front of me. I take her in—from her luscious breasts to her tiny waist to her captivating fucking hips and legs until my greedy regard finds her pussy.

"Brook, do you have any idea what I'm about to do to you?"

Her eyes light up, big and bold, luring me in even further.

Not waiting for her to answer, I drop to my knees. "You have the prettiest fucking pussy."

I have no intention of stopping there. I've only just begun.

"Your scent is fucking addictive. You know that?"

Her breathing hitches, waiting for my next move.

Her legs tremble.

Her body shakes.

Her hips sway, baiting me to continue.

"How should I make you wet first? Should it be with my fingers? My mouth? Tell me how I should make you come."

"Any way you want me ..."

She moans as I slide two fingers inside her warm, welcoming heat.

"I'm going to make you come down my hand by finger fucking you right ... here." I push on her G-spot, not letting up. Her head falls back with her leg on my shoulder.

"Ronan... please..."

"Begging me won't give you mercy. If anything, it only triggers me to do the opposite. Now the question is, should I make you come or make you wait? Because all I have to do is push back farther and hit ... right ... here..."

"Oh God! Don't stop... Please ... right there ... don't stop..."

"You feel that, Brook? That's me finger fucking your

G-spot." Moving my fingers back and forth, I get right up in there.

Faster.

Harder.

I give her everything I have.

With the palm of my other hand, I stimulate her clit from side to side, never letting up on my assault inside her.

"Yeah... just like that..."

It doesn't take long for her to do exactly that, screaming, "Ronan!" in pure abandonment. She comes so fucking hard, she almost pushes my fingers out.

I allow her to ride the wave of ecstasy before huskily groaning, "Now we can get to my favorite part."

"What?"

Our eyes connect.

What started off as tender becomes rough and demanding.

"I'm going to fuck you with my tongue."

I slide it into her pussy as far as it will go. Still playing with her swollen, sensitive nub, I manipulate it with the palm of my hand until she comes in the back of my throat.

The salty sweetness of her cum is delicious.

My dick throbs to the point of pain, so I unzip my slacks and pull out my cock. I instantly stroke it up and down as she watches through a hooded gaze while I eat her out.

She goes crazy with desire, cuming so goddamn hard again. Her juices drip down my face and throat, and I love every second of it. She even drenches the top of my button-down shirt. Locking my other arm around her thighs, I hold her down against the wall behind her.

She's squirming, begging for mercy. Her breathing is heavy and deep, and her skin is bright pink and shimmers with a light film of sweat. She shines bright with the afterglow of her orgasms.

I'll never tire of watching her come undone.

She's fucking breathtaking.

Letting her rest for a couple of seconds, I wipe my mouth with the back of my hand and lick the rest from my lips, savoring it in my mouth for as long as I can. While I stand, I lick my fingers and show her exactly what she's doing to me before I stick them in her mouth and make her lick them clean for me.

In one swift movement, I grip her thighs and slam her against the wall as I thrust my dick deep inside her. She jolts forward, feeling the impact of my cock. Her lips drop into a gorgeous "o" and her eyes go half lidded as I pull out deliciously slowly and then swiftly thrust up, filling her and fucking her like she's mine to play with. Her nails dig into my shoulders as she holds me, fueling me to fuck her faster.

"You feel ..." she moans, "so fucking big, Professor Wolf."

"Words every man loves to hear."

To prove my point, I pull out and slam back into her, which causes her body to inch higher on the white wall.

The feel of her cunt.

The taste of her cum.

The smell of her arousal.

My mind's reeling with so many conflicting emotions that I can't keep up with them. There's so much I want to say, but I barely understand what's wreaking havoc on my mind. I want to remember her just this way for the rest of the day. Her long hair spread all over her face. Her slightly flushed cheeks, and the blush creeping down her neck. How her lips are swollen from my touch, and her serene eyes glaze over.

So beautiful.

So captivating.

Everything I didn't know I could have until this moment.

I love seeing every emotion I feel through her gaze as I thrust in and out of her pussy. Her bright eyes watch me passionately as I take what I need.

What she's giving me.

Her body shudders. Her pussy fits me like a glove.

Tight.

Wet.

Warm.

I can come right then and there, but I want to feel more of her. Gripping her waist, I slam in and out of her, getting as far as I can inside her.

"Yeah, Brooklyn, just like that."

She lets go, almost taking me with her. Hugging around

her neck, I kiss her, Our mouths fuse, unable to get enough of one another. It seems like hours pass, and the whole world is left behind us.

If only we can be so lucky.

"Ronan..." she moans. Her pussy pulsates around my shaft, clamping down hard.

It feels so good. I thrust in and out a few more times until I can't hold back any longer and lose myself deep inside her.

CHAPTER 7

BROOKLYN

My fingertips play along my lips, and my body heats instantly at his memory. I quickly put my hand back in my lap and glance around. It's not like anyone in this café courtyard will know what I'm thinking, but the very thought of that kiss from Ro feels like a sin, and I will be judged for it.

My lips, my throat, every little bit of me.

He kissed me like I was his to do with what he pleased, and I fucking loved it. He's lucky I didn't smack him, though, and that his arrogant ass left before I could wrap my head around what had happened.

It's either I'm truly fucked up for loving this tension with him, or it's some kind of avoidance of reality. Like I'm into

Ro just so I can deny what we did was wrong. I imagine my old therapist, who gave up on me, would say something like that. I'm not sure exactly what she'd say, to be honest, or what buzzwords would come out of her mouth. I know what I'd tell her, though.

My body is at war with logic and reason, and my heart is a treacherous bitch. It's that simple. I'm fucked.

My phone dings with a text message, and I don't have to wonder who it is.

Aspen: *You said you'd call.*

Brooklyn: *I will.*

Aspen: *I'm freaking out, and I don't understand. What the hell is going on?*

I leave her on read and try not to even think about the fact that no one else has messaged me. They all know. They've all seen. But no one else has messaged me. A tingle makes my fingers go numb as the server sets down a cup of tea in a porcelain saucer, complete with edible flower petals floating on top.

I get it. Things like this are a trickle and then a flood. They're waiting to see the fallout. I've been here before.

It's to be expected, I tell myself, then have another sip and pretend it doesn't hurt. Instead of thinking anything at all, I look up and take a deep breath.

The high-end café is gorgeous. I love the energy and

ambience of all the colors and patterns in the room. Not to mention, all the people enjoying their day like I'm still desperately trying to. Except I can't. I'm about to meet my father, and I know it will cut the last string I've been holding on to today.

I try to focus on the ambience and allow the good vibes to take over until I'm distracted by the server again. After thanking her, I pluck the petals out like the little menaces they are and imagine they're each one of those little bitches who are absolutely talking about me behind my back rather than to my face. The back of my eyes sting, imagining what they're saying, but I honestly can't give a fuck at the moment.

Although I'm grateful it hasn't been leaked to the press.

Yet.

I won't put it past them to leak it themselves. Everyone wants to be Queen B, which means cutting down everyone else any chance they give you. And I'm sure this opportunity is far too tempting.

As my rage and anger and the feeling of betrayal threaten to make me spiral, I grip the hot cup of chamomille tea with both hands and sip.

Deep breath.

I swallow thickly, barely tasting the beverage.

My most awful thought is that, hopefully, my father can fix this. As if he ever would. I can already hear him telling me I need to suffer the consequences even though I'm the one who's been violated. On that thought, my phone pings.

Aspen: Seriously??? You're just going to ignore me?

Brooklyn: *I'm not ignoring you. Just barely holding on. I want to know who sent the video.*

Aspen: *I don't know, but your dad can find out, can't he?*

I don't answer, sick to my stomach over her response, and it's then I glance at the time and realize it's ten after. He's ten minutes late, and he's never late. I think he's blowing me off.

Just as my emotions threaten, Aspen texts again.

Aspen: *Or Ronan can.*

Is it really between my father and the arrogant dick Professor Wolf? Those two men are my only hope? I hate relying on anyone. As hypocritical as it is. I wish I could just ask my father for a contact, but he'd do it himself and keep me reliant on him. He always has.

Aspen: *Just so you know, I was thinking about making moves, but he never did. I was wondering why he wouldn't flirt back, and I guess it's a good thing it's because of you. Even if you're a b for not telling me about the two of you getting engaged. When did you start dating, and why didn't you trust me with it?*

I start to write "it's not what it looks like," then delete

it. I know better than to put damning evidence into writing when my ass is on the line, but I quickly think about the text exchanges with Ronan earlier, and I suddenly run cold.

Shit.

Brooklyn: *I'll tell you about it later.*

Aspen texts something, but I don't get a chance to see what she wrote. My father's shadow hovers above me, and I barely manage to look him in the eyes.

"Daughter," he states slowly with spite as he pulls out the metal bistro chair, dragging its legs against the stone floor.

"Father." I barely manage to keep myself from imitating his tone. "I was beginning to think you blew me off and weren't coming."

"I was debating on it."

I swallow thickly, barely keeping his gaze, but I keep it. I'm not surprised by his response. I'd be lying if I said I didn't think about it too.

The server approaches, and before she can even greet him, he waves her off without even looking at her. She turns on her heels, her brunette hair swaying with a brisk wind as she does. The chill and the turn of weather are apt, given the contempt on my father's face. I feel bad for her. She didn't sully his name. She's just doing her job. I glance back at him, and it's like he can read my thoughts. Sickness stirs in my gut, and I look back at my tea.

He stares at me in silence. I'm used to it. He wears the look of betrayal so well. He's nailed it down perfectly since my mother left him. I used to resent her for leaving, but I get it in a way.

"Well, I'm glad you came." I attempt to be civil, but he continues to stare. "I'm in need of help." Again, I get nothing. It's like he doesn't even see me, or what he sees is so very beneath him that I'm practically invisible.

"I want to know who sent the video." I don't bother to wait for any niceties or sympathy from him.

"Is your fiancé not hiring a detective?" he asks, and the way he says the word fiancé makes my skin crawl.

My gaze falters. I look down at his fists on the table, and I know he knows I'm lying. His black suit only adds to his intense composure as I think about the consequences if I tell him the truth.

How pissed will Ronan be?

A war inside me rages, and all it does is make me sick. I hate all of this.

I don't want him to lose his chance at tenure, let alone his job. He's worked hard for it, and who am I to take that away from him. I can't bring myself to do it. I can't bring myself to betray him, so I deceive my father instead. Although I know it's a futile effort.

How fucked up is that?

The thing is, he'll find out. There's no privacy with a man like my father. Every little lie will crash down around me. I already know it and just want all of this to disappear. So again, I consider telling him the truth.

At this moment of weakness, I contemplate confessing because I need the thoughts in my head to stop. I've spiraled before, and I know how this ends. Even though this feels worse. It feels heavier, and I don't know how I'll make it out of this if I'm forced to go alone. I don't want to feel like this. My father might make me feel worse for a moment. He might call me names and say awful things, but he'll make it go away.

"Fiancé," I murmur as I pick up my cup of tea. All the while, a small voice in the back of my head screams for me to just tell him because it'll be worse when he discovers the truth. I stare blankly at the cup, trying to figure out how to tell him while also protecting Ronan. It's a delicate situation, given that Ro could lose his entire life over this.

I decide I just need more time to think.

"Your penthouse... is no longer yours," my father states, interrupting my thoughts and causing my blood to run cold.

I blink at him, taken aback. "Excuse me?"

Certain things were split during their divorce, but since they were done, certain assets go to me. It's mine. Or at least I was given that impression.

"Your allowance as well," he says so easily, so definitively, like he hasn't just stripped away all I've ever known. Allowance?

That's not what a trust is. Meetings with the lawyers race in my head, but all they do at this moment is question what I know about the law and the contracts I was told to sign.

My blood runs cold.

"You can't do that," I practically hiss as my hands attempt a fist, and my nails dig into my skin. My heart races, and adrenaline pumps through my veins as I realize what he's doing. "You're cutting me off?" I say like it's a question, but it's not. I know exactly what he's trying to accomplish, and in the end, he'll win.

He always wins whether I want him to or not. My mother is the only person who has ever given him a taste of his own medicine.

She's strong.

Brave.

Not like me.

Despite being an adult, I still feel like I'm just a helpless little girl in his presence. I wish I could break the powerful hold he has over me, and now he's simply stripping me of everything.

"But you should be fine, shouldn't you?" he coaxes, feigning concern as he leans back in his chair. Another gust of chilled air comes by, and I shiver, wishing I'd brought a coat. "You have your fiancé, after all."

There's a thump in my chest, almost like hopelessness. Ronan asked me what I wanted. He wanted to make a deal. I swallow down the emotions coming over me, and I square my shoulders as I look at my father.

I decide right then and there to play this game with both of them.

"I'm sure my fiancé wasn't expecting my finances to change drastically, but I'll inform him of the change, and his counsel can advise me on any legal actions that should be taken."

My father's eyes narrow, and he leans forward. "Are you threatening me?"

I meet his stance, lacing my fingers in front of me as I lean forward. Almost whispering, I say, "Father, I thought we were here to discuss the person who violated your only daughter and her fiancé with that recording... so were you here for something else?"

Feigning ignorance and accepting his punishment without a fight, he fucking hates when I do that. And just like he always does, he storms off, huffing something under his breath that I don't quite catch.

He loves to get to me.

He can eat shit.

Only after he leaves do I look down at my phone and read what Aspen sent.

Aspen: *You better, B, cause this is bad.*

I reflect on her text, then tuck my phone back into my purse before I get the hell out of there, realizing just how bad this truly is.

CHAPTER 8

RONAN

The day flies by, and suddenly, the office in my home is filled with only the dim light cascading through the curtains of the large bay window. I'm exhausted. I've spent the entire day trying to figure out who the fuck recorded us and why they sent it to the board. I can't help but think about what they truly want and why they're playing a seedy hand.

Who the hell knew we would be there? Brooklyn insists no one knew she'd be there. Given that they initially sent it to the board, it's someone out to get me. God knows I've made enemies, and whoever it is won't stop. That's the only truth I know as I run my hand down my face and grit my teeth.

I hate not being in control and not being able to use

my connections or money to find out the truth in a matter of seconds. They should fucking know. I've given them everything, and they've given me nothing. The detective should have given me a name, address, and the fucking social security number of the prick who sent that email. Instead, I'm waiting like a fucking idiot for the other shoe to drop. I can't imagine it ends here. If anything, this is only the beginning.

I wait for a call.

A note.

Maybe another email demanding money or some sort of ransom not to show the world that explicit video of us. Nothing makes sense, and the more I try to understand, the less I feel like I do. I'm torn and confused about where we go from here, and all I can do is pray that I'm doing the right thing by trusting that woman.

I still don't have full faith that it wasn't her in the first place... She's never been in my bar before. She's never hit on me before. I'm brought back to that night and the way she eye fucked me from down the bar before ordering me a glass of whiskey. Fuck, even exhausted and burned out, I'm hard as a rock remembering that moment I knew she wanted me the way I wanted her. But why would she do that to herself? It doesn't make any sense.

I rack my brain for hours on who it can be and how I can find out the truth behind this motherfucker who has this hanging over my head.

Have I fucked anyone over?

Now, that's a loaded question if I've ever heard one. As much as I can say I'm a successful businessman, I've also fucked people over in the process. Her father being the top name on that list. You don't get where I am in life without fucking a handful of people over to get there. You know what they say, it's lonely at the top, and I can attest to that. I don't have many friends or people I can trust.

I grew up looking out for myself, and that's it. My father made sure of it, but it made me a man. I don't have a relationship with him or my mother anymore, and I'm the only child. This is just how I've lived my life. It's easier not having to worry about anyone but me.

The wind picks up outside, and the second I feel the shift in the atmosphere, I hear what can only be the front door of my home open and then close. Nobody has the key.

Slowly, I grab my gun from inside the drawer and make my way to the disruption. Step by step, I move on autopilot, trying to get to the bottom of who the fuck just let themselves inside my home uninvited. It's dark, so I can barely see with a looming migraine forming in the forefront of my mind.

My palms are sweaty as I call out, "Who's there?"

Shaking away the unease, I'm met with a shadow in front of me. Fucking hell.

In one breath, I warn, "You got a death wish?" My heart races as I instantly lower the gun.

I'm hit with the scent of Brooklyn's vanilla shampoo as I swiftly turn her around to face me. Her eyes are as wide as saucers when she locks her stare with mine.

She teases, "Paranoid much?"

"Says the woman who just broke into my home." Moving back to my desk, I put the gun back, noting she knows where it's kept now.

"I didn't break in, asshole. I used your key."

I cock my head to the side. I usually come in through the garage. "What key?"

"The one I stole off your keychain this morning after you arrogantly kissed me without my consent."

She's testing my patience, and I don't feel like I have any left at the moment. Especially when it comes to her.

"You want to talk about consent? You're here uninvited after you stole my key."

"I'm your fiancée, remember? I thought what's yours is mine, Professor Wolf."

I huff a humorless laugh. "That's not at all what that means."

"Well, my father always says I have no sense. Particularly when it comes to my choice of men."

I half smile, nodding. "What do you want, Brooklyn?"

She flicks on the light and walks into my living room like she owns the damn place. The red knee-length dress she's wearing sways, and the view of her ass eases the tension in my body. Red is definitely her color. It's made for her, and I make a mental note of that. I'll never get over the air about her. She's fucking gorgeous, but there's something else. She clears her throat, turning to face me, and says, "My father is cutting me off."

We lock eyes.

"I have nothing if I keep this charade going." She attempts to keep her tone even, but I hear the hitch in her voice. "I'm here to tell you, I can't help you. We have to tell the truth and call the whole thing off."

"The fuck we do."

"Did you not hear what I just said? I have nothing, and I can't play house with you." Her voice almost cracks as if she's on edge. I swallow thickly. He really fucking cut her off? Or is this a lie? A trick?

I pause a moment and then say, "Don't worry about it."

"Don't worry about it?" she mocks. "What exactly shouldn't I be worrying about? The fact that I won't have a place to live or the fact that I won't have money to eat? How should I not worry about that?"

"You said we had a deal."

"That was before my father wanted to take everything away from me. What am I supposed to do, huh? Crash on your couch?"

"I'd much rather have you in my bed."

"Excuse me?" Her chest rises and falls as she stares back at me in disbelief.

"You heard me."

"I don't think I did." She contemplates it for a second. "What do you mean in your bed?"

"You're my fiancée. What's mine is yours," I repeat her words from minutes ago. "I'll give you whatever you need."

I anticipate a retort or even backlash from my teasing, but she responds far too seriously.

"For how long?"

"For as long as it takes." I look her up and down. It's real. There's no doubt it's real, and he cut her off.

"As long as what takes?"

Not hesitating, I grab my wallet and hand her my black Amex card. She looks at it, then at me with a skeptical yet relieved expression.

"Just like that?"

"You'll live here with me, and you can use that card for whatever you need."

She looks at it a moment longer. "What about for what I want?"

My lips pick up in an asymmetric smile.

"Be my little whore, and I don't give a fuck what you do as long as you hold up your end of the deal." It should alarm me how much I mean that. I don't keep girlfriends. I spoil an interest here and there, but giving them free rein with my wealth and allowing them to keep a key?

Never.

"Your whore?" she echoes back as if it's offensive.

"My good little whore?" I offer in feigned clarification.

"You're an asshole," she roars, stomping her foot like it threatens me.

I scoff out a chuckle instead. "But you're tempted?"

"Yes. I am tempted, but what happens after our deal is over? Where does that leave me? If my father cuts me off, I have no reassurance of getting it back once we're done pretending to be husband and wife."

"You can't tell anyone the truth. It stays between me and you."

Her eyes narrow, and I know she's questioning whether she should keep our arrangement a secret. "Not to anyone. Not to your father or to Aspen or—"

"You're asking me to lie to my best friend?"

"I'm asking you to lie to everyone." I stress the word.

She swallows hard and nods for my answer to her initial question.

"Don't you have a trust fund?"

"Not until I'm twenty-five, and it's null and void if I get married before that."

I state, "That's three years from now."

She smirks, realizing I know more about her than she gives me credit for.

"We aren't going to keep this up for three years," she states although her eyes reflect that she desperately needs that trust and security until she's financially secure. How the hell can her own father do this to her?

"I would think not, but we can arrange something so you don't have to worry."

She nods although she seems uncertain.

"So do we have a deal?"

Her cautious gaze shifts toward the ceiling as if she's waiting for an answer from God.

"What do I get out of this?" she finally asks.

"What do you want?"

"If I'm getting cut off, then I want a settlement when we split."

"How much?"

"A million."

It doesn't surprise me that she demands this much. She probably spends that in a month. She has no sense of value for anything. I have millions in stocks alone with my own trust fund. My bar is the best in town, and it makes tons of revenue. And even it is pennies compared to what the brokerage account makes.

For a second, I contemplate the alternative before I rasp, "Done."

She smiles. "I want a contract in writing."

"I'll have one for you in the morning."

She crosses her arms over her chest. "Now what?"

"Now you get on your knees and thank me."

She sasses, "Or what?"

"You can..." Looking her up and down with a predatory regard, I add, "Come here and kiss me."

CHAPTER 9

BROOKLYN

His home is a bachelor pad if I've ever seen one. No one will believe I live here. I continue to glance around while we're eating breakfast the following morning. After we came to an agreement, I took a bath in his massive tub, thinking he'd join me in bed, but he didn't.

I didn't see him for the rest of the night, and then this morning, he's standing in the kitchen bright-eyed and bushy-tailed with my coffee in his hand. Someone delivered us breakfast, and now we're sitting on opposite ends of his long rectangular dining table like we're in a business meeting. In a way, I guess we are.

I have to keep reminding myself that this isn't real. We're

not in love and engaged. It's all a facade. However, when he's looking at me with that devilish stare, and his tantalizing green eyes stare into my soul, it's hard to distinguish between fact and fiction.

My parents never showed much love for each other, and my father always worked. From an early age, I promised myself I'd never be in a loveless marriage, but here I am, playing the part of his fiancée as if this is my very own version of a fucked-up Pretty Woman.

I want to ask him where he went last night because I looked for him. This place isn't that large, and I didn't see him anywhere before I climbed back into bed. I desperately want to know where he went and if he was with someone.

Out of nowhere, he interrupts my reckless thoughts, stating, "We should throw an engagement party, and by we, I mean you." As I stare back at him, he tends to his eggs Benedict. His black coffee sends a gust of steam into the air, and I realize he's serious.

"How lovely. I've always wanted to have no input from my future husband. If we're going to have an engagement party, then I'll need to redecorate."

"What am I missing? I don't have enough pink pillows and throw blankets for you?"

"As a matter of fact, you don't have any pillows or throw blankets, so yes. It needs to look like I live here too, and right now, it only screams a place where you bring women to fuck."

My fork scrapes against the plate as I scoop up a bit of hollandaise and eggs. Perfectly cooked.

"Rest assured, my little whore, I've never brought a woman here before."

Shocked, I jerk back. "You're lying."

"What need do I have to lie to you?"

I take a sip of my coffee, and as I'm setting it back down on the table, I respond, "Then where do you fuck them?"

"The same place I fucked you."

I'm hurt.

Deeply.

Profoundly.

Undeniably hurt by his reply.

I don't know why, though. It's honestly silly and stupid. Of course, I'm not the first woman he's fucked on his bar.

I must have made a face since he asks, "That upsets you?"

I quickly recover, returning to the woman who hides it all. Especially her feelings.

"Don't flatter yourself, Professor Wolf." I go back to my breakfast although I have no appetite at all now.

"Your expression tells another story."

"If by that you mean my surprise? I guess I thought you wouldn't be that careless to be caught on video like you were with me."

"It was a joke, Brooklyn," he says, and I tell him it wasn't funny. I almost ask him then where do you fuck the women you're seeing, but I keep my mouth shut. I don't want to know. I regret ever asking.

I glance up at him as I take a sip of coffee, and his expression shows slight remorse. How can he possibly think that was funny. Fucking prick.

"I'm sorry."

"For what? Fucking me and dragging me into this new nightmare so you can make jokes?" There's enough bite in my tone to leave a scar, and I fucking hope it does.

"I don't usually fuck students." His tone is different, and I can't place it.

"Usually?" I counter. "And I'm not your student."

"You know what I mean."

"I obviously don't."

Inhaling a deep, rapid breath, he calms himself and then retorts, "You can redecorate whatever you want except my office."

"That's fair."

"Thanks for being so understanding, considering this is my place after all." He offers a thin smile.

"Not when I'm done with it."

He opens his mouth to say something, but the doorbell cuts him off.

He arches an eyebrow, and I answer his silent demand. "It's Aspen," I say as I push the chair out. "My best friend. I invited her." And she's going to hear about your fucking standup comedy, you fucking prick, I think as I head to the door.

"I know who Aspen is and what she is to you."

I resist the urge to ask him how much he knows about me until he abruptly stands and excuses himself to his office. Quick on my feet, I hustle toward the door and open it.

Before I can greet her, she spews, "What the fuck is going on?"

I gesture to the open floor plan. "I want to redecorate."

She's an interior decorator. So perfect timing.

"Brooklyn, what the hell?"

"Come on." I grab her hand. "Let me show you around."

"Where's Ronan?" she asks, and I say I don't give a shit. Her expression scrunches, and I ignore it, closing the door and deciding that I don't need breakfast. I need to spend a fuck ton of money on art that I plan to replace next week. Now, the expression on his face when he gets the bill? That will be fucking funny.

She goes along with what I have to say and all my ideas on what I want to do with the place until we're sitting out on the balcony, and she demands to know what is happening. Since I can't tell her the truth, I make up a story about how we started dating and why I couldn't tell her.

"I was just accepted into the program, and we were more concerned about his job than telling anyone, you know?" I nod, and she nods along with me. I fucking hope she believes me. Even if I hate myself for lying to her.

Even though she listens to every word I have to say, I can tell by her expression that she wants to call bullshit. But she knows I won't tell her the truth unless I want to, and the fact of the matter is, I can't.

I've already told him I won't, and I can't risk him kicking me out on my ass too. I hate lying to her, but I have no choice. I've never lied to Aspen before, and I hate that this is happening in the first place.

"So because you're a student, you had to keep your relationship a secret? You know I'd never tell anyone, Brook."

"I know, but Ronan is paranoid and about to make tenure, so we wanted to wait to tell everyone until after he did. With the video, we were forced to come clean. He asked me to marry him last week."

She eyes me skeptically, then looks down at my hand. "Where's your ring?"

"It's getting sized."

"He didn't know your ring size?"

"He's a man, Aspen."

She arches a brow and crosses her arms over her chest. "Good point."

I lean against the iron railing, embracing the cool breeze. Thank God she's accepting what I'm telling her.

"How does your father feel about the two of you?"

The pain of yesterday comes back tenfold. I swallow and decide to push every emotion down and just shrug. "It doesn't matter. I'm happy, and I get to spend a shit ton of money while still pissing my father off. I call that a win." She's my best friend, and I can't bring myself to tell her.

"Are you staying in school, then?"

"I might." I answer and realize I haven't even thought about it. I wonder if I quit school if they will even care that Ronan and I are engaged… and what that would mean about the deal I just made with him. Fuck. It's a web of lies.

"What plans do you have for the future? Where are you getting married? Do you want kids?"

Her questions go on and on, and I try to answer each one to the best of my ability. Ronan steps out onto the balcony, and his presence instantly demands attention which he radiates twenty-four seven.

He greets her. "Good morning, Aspen."

She smiles. "Good morning, Professor Wolf." He huffs a laugh as if genuinely amused.

"I'm sure Brooklyn has caught you all up?" he asks before taking a gulp of coffee. I notice his eyes never leave her, though.

"Yeah." She nervously chuckles. "She's just full of surprises these days. I guess a congratulation is in order."

"Don't worry about it." In two strides, Ronan grips my waist and pulls me toward him as if I belong to him. Seconds later, he's kissing me like we're not in front of my best friend. Obviously, he has something to prove.

My knees buckle, and my chest tightens, enjoying the feel of being wrapped in his arms. It's not until he pulls back and looks deep into my eyes that I find it hard to breathe. And even harder to remember what lies I've just told Aspen and what lies I want to tell myself.

CHAPTER 10

RONAN

What the fuck?

I'm frozen in place as the penthouse door closes behind me with a loud thud. My gaze moves slowly across the living room and into the kitchen. Every little fucking thing has her hand on it.

Heat creeps up the back of my neck. How in the hell is it even possible to change everything in less than eight hours?

A new chandelier dangles straight ahead of me, and I stay utterly fucking still as my jaw clenches. I hired not "one of the top" but the top designer to decorate my place over six years ago when I first got my position, and in a single day, Brook has transformed every last inch of it.

All my furniture has been replaced, and as I continue to look around, I see that everything has been replaced. She's altered it all as if it were truly hers to change. I don't recognize a foot in front of me while I inspect a space that looks more like a home now. I go through each room, simply taking it in and attempting to remain calm. There's even fresh paint on the once gray walls. They're all off-white now, with flower wallpaper in the bathrooms.

All I see are dollar signs in the dainty pillows that read of luxury and the paintings that line the back wall as if she's having a go at seeing which of the ones selected she prefers. Adrenaline courses through my veins. There are mirrors with gold trim and a gilded coffee table I wouldn't live with if my fucking life depended on it.

"It's called mineral tones," she says from my left.

Every thought of the decor vanishes when I spot Brooklyn donning what can only be described as a schoolgirl slut costume. Her nylons are pulled into place with clips and a solid, thin line that runs down her legs.

She adds, "It's uptown chic with a feminine flair."

"Is that right?" I question, barely hearing a word as I take in the button that's holding on for dear life between her breasts.

My cock is instantly hard, and no amount of blood remains for logical thought.

Fuck the wall color. It's not like I give a shit anyway.

Swallowing thickly, I rake my eyes down her gorgeous

curves, then back up to her gaze. I can't help but smile as the mischievousness shines in her doe eyes. It dawns on me. This is her revenge. A chess piece moved. I suppress a smirk. If one day of shopping can get me off the hook for the dumb shit I say without thinking, she can have every fucking penny.

"What's this?" I murmur as I toss my suitcase on the new-to-me chaise lounge and loosen my tie.

"I hope you like it, Professor Wolf," she says seductively, and I swear to God, she must've practiced that line. "I bought it for you."

My cock is so fucking hard that I leak precum.

I have to close my eyes and stifle a groan.

What this woman does to me is sinful.

When I open them, I attempt to right myself. Her blond hair shines with the new dimmed light from the chandelier, and I'll be damned, but she's never looked better.

Well... maybe when she was tied up and under me. I'll never get over that.

"What are you doing, Brook?"

"I've always had a professor kink," she says, taking a hesitant step forward as her fingers play with the hem of her dangerously short plaid skirt. "And I've been a bad girl." Her pouty lips beg me to kiss her, but I stand exactly where I am.

"What did you do?" I ask her, ignoring the throbbing ache in my cock.

She smirks at me so fucking devilishly. She's sin in black

heels with fuck-me eyes, and I can barely contain myself.

"You don't want to know how much I spent," she murmurs, and that little vixen look comes over her. "You should make sure you're getting your money's worth."

Her last comment breaks me out of my spell, and I force myself to avert my eyes as I remove my jacket and drape it neatly across the back of the wingback chair.

I smooth over it as I ask her, "Are you ready for class?"

"Why, yes, I am—" She uses that same playful teasing tone, and I cut her off.

"No, your classes. Your real classes," I stress, knowing damn well I don't trust this, and I don't trust her.

I'm only half concerned with how much she spent and more concerned with what else she'll change without telling me.

She shrugs it off, then parts her lips as if she'll give me some excuse.

"You need to attend your classes," I stress.

Her lips straighten to a thin line before she says, "I don't see why I should go. I was only doing it because of my father, and I blocked him today, so..."

"You blocked him?" My forehead is tight with the crease from my scrunched brow.

"Yes. I hit the button on the phone that says—" she responds as if I can't fucking comprehend how to block someone.

"I know what blocked means," I grit out, barely holding

back my irritation. My heart pounds. I hate that she's one of them. "What are you doing, Brooklyn?"

"What does it look like?" she says once again, playing dumb. She's anything but, and she damn well knows that I know that.

For a moment, her eyes reflect the shock and grief she's been holding back.

There she is... the version of her I met in the bar that night. The raw, vulnerable woman who wanted to escape, and I found myself there, wanting the same.

"You're smarter than this," I say as I take another step toward her.

She stares at me, her eyes wide as if she knows I can really see her for who she is. The real her. She steps back, her knees hitting the other chair and preventing her from moving. I know she's hurt, and for a moment, a moment, I think she may walk away.

Not just from this moment but from all of it.

Me included.

I can't fucking risk that. I need her. More than she knows.

"Get on your knees." My hands land on my belt buckle, and I wait for her to move.

She swallows hard, meeting my eyes as a smirk spreads across her lips.

"Come on, my little whore, get on your knees for me like the good girl you are."

She doesn't move, not one step. She wants me to come to her instead. This is a battle, an all-out war of who controls the other more.

Hours, minutes, seconds could have rolled by, and I give her what she wants in the end because I can't resist her. As much as I crave to, as much as I pray to, as much as I hope to.

I just can't let her go.

Dammit all to hell.

In one long stride, I turn her back to my front to whisper in her ear from behind her, "I need you to be good for me."

I can feel it in her stance that she wants to defy me. Except she can't. She likes being at my mercy too much, bending to my will.

She winks at me with a quick glance over her shoulder before she drops to her knees. In another swift motion, she has my throbbing hard cock in her tiny grasp, working me over hard and fast.

"Fuck..." I rasp, never breaking eye contact with her. I have to brace myself with a hand on the wall.

Goddamn.

She slides my cock into her mouth like it was made for only her, deep throating it until I can feel the back of her throat, and her cheeks hollow. Fucking gorgeous. I grip the hair on the nape of her neck, gliding her up and down my shaft until she gags.

I don't give her a chance to recover and catch her breath

before I tear my dick out of her pouty fuck-me lips and place her where I want her. Right against the back of the couch, I press her body forward. As I pull up her short skirt, I slap her ass, and I love her yelp. In less than a second, I thrust my cock inside her.

Fucking hell, she feels like heaven. I focus on the sweet moans that pour from her lips. My thrusts are deep and relentless, and she takes each of them while her nails scratch against the sofa until she grips a pillow.

She nearly cries out her pleasure into it, but I can't fucking have that. I want to hear every sound.

I pull her head back, my hand on her throat, to kiss that luscious mouth of hers, all needy and wet from my assault. She purrs and sucks on my tongue like she just did my dick as I roughly pound into her now soaking wet cunt.

"Yessss... Professor Wolf. God, yessss..."

I growl, digging my fingers into her hips as her pussy tightens on my cock like she's trying to choke the shit out of it.

Mine.

"You're my little whore... tell me you know that."

When she doesn't answer, I fuck her harder and demand it again. Her lips drop into a perfect "o," and it's the sexiest fucking thing I've ever seen.

"I'm your little whore, Professor Wolf," she whimpers.

Moaning.

Panting.

The sound of my balls slapping her cunt echoes off the walls around us.

She comes, and it doesn't take long for her to drag me over the edge with her. I know she's on birth control, so I don't think twice about coming deep inside her.

After we're done, I carry her to my bed. I guess at this point, it's our bed, and I lay her down next to me.

Her chest is still rising and falling with the waves of her pleasure. Hell, even I'm still on a high, but I take advantage of the moment.

"We'll have to establish some ground rules."

She glances over at me, tucking her arm under her head to look at me. "Rules are made to be broken."

"I'm serious."

"So am I."

"You're going to school, or else it will only cause more suspicion about our engagement." I search the bedroom for a pair of boxers as I talk.

She watches me as I pull a pair on. "That sounds like bullshit." Naked under that sheet, she tempts me.

"And I want you in my class at the end of the day." I climb into the end of the bed and keep her gaze.

"Professor Wolf," she mocks, her cheeks still flushed and with a look in her eyes that I love. "What if we get caught?" she teases.

"Jesus, Brook, I just want to kiss you and get used to it

outside of a fucking bedroom or restaurant bar."

She laughs a bit, then looks away. A moment passes, and the air changes.

"How are you doing with all of this?" I ask.

She shrugs. "As well as I can be."

Reality slowly comes back, and I decide to confide in her. "I have a PI looking into this. I'll get to the bottom of this."

"It doesn't matter anyway. People already have a clear opinion about me."

"And what's that?"

"Don't act like you don't already know what it is."

"Try me."

She rolls her eyes. "People think I'm just a spoiled little rich girl with daddy issues who sleeps around."

"Who's people?"

She glances at me. "Everyone we know." I fucking doubt they all know, but obviously something happened.

I try my hand at flattery. "I thought everyone wanted to be Brooklyn Chambers?"

She huffs. "They might, but that doesn't change what they think about me." She picks at an invisible thread on the sheets.

There's so much I want to say to her, but I hold back. I can't give her what she needs to hear. I still don't trust her.

Instead, I lean closer and softly kiss her. "All that matters is what you think about yourself."

Her eyes narrow before I add, "We're going to the charity event, so make sure you have a dress for that."

"I don't have any of my dresses."

"Why not?"

She stares at me like I haven't read whatever memo she sent me. "He changed the locks."

"Your father changed the locks?" The anger that rises inside me is irrational, yet…

She nods. "I can't get the rest of my things, so I have to go shopping. Woe is me, right?"

Despite her trying to make it come out as a joke, she's simply trying to hide her real emotions from me. Not that I blame her. She doesn't trust me either.

"Your father's a prick."

She shrugs again and pulls out a vape from the bedside table. "You want a hit?"

My brow arches as I watch her suck in and then blow out a puff. "I'm too old for that shit."

"That's right," she teases. "You're what? Pushing forty?"

"You little shit." I kiss her cheek and leave her to her weed and emotions before running her a bath and ordering her to take one.

I can see in her eyes that she wants to thank me, and she does… by standing in front of me. She shrieks and jumps into the water the second I reach for her. I resist the urge to follow her because I have work to do. Once I'm in my office, I text my lawyer and tell him he needs to find a way to get all her shit from her dad's place.

Ronan: *I don't give a shit how you get her stuff. Break in if you have to. Just make sure it's done. He can't lock her out without notice. It's against the law. If he wants to fuck with her...*

I don't hesitate in adding...

Ronan: *Then he's fucking with me.*

CHAPTER 11

BROOKLYN

The bed groans, and I'm forced to groan too as I turn over and feel the soreness between my legs. Ro did a number on me last night, and I fucking loved it. I hide my smile into the pillow just in case he's watching. Every intimate moment with him just keeps getting better and better. I have to continue reminding myself that this is all fake.

We aren't engaged.

He doesn't love me.

This is all pretend.

We're playing house, and I'm praying I don't burn it down before this is all said and done.

I want to do what he asks, but it's like I'm giving up all my power to him, and it's getting scarily easy to do. I'm far too happy to just forget. I love what he does to me too much. I know this will be over sooner rather than later, so I can't get too used to his hands on me.

His mouth on me.

His cock inside me.

It's all for show.

We're nothing but an illusion that's become a reality for the sole purpose of covering his ass so he doesn't get fired. I never thought this could happen, and I'd be lying if I said I didn't like it.

I didn't like him.

Be strong, Brooklyn. You're a means to an end.

The warmth that floods my cheek slips down south, but I'm met with a loss as I realize I'm alone. His side of the bed is cold.

I sit up in bed. How long has he been gone?

My smile slips into a pout, and I rub the sleep from my eyes as I gather the sheets around me to keep the chill away. Then I realize it's darker than before in the morning... darker because something's blocking the windows.

It takes me a minute longer than it should because of the disbelief. I sit up straighter, rechecking my surroundings as my heart hammers and every little event comes back to me.

There's a rack in his room. It's my rack of designer dresses. The dresses I thought I would never see again. My eyes widen.

Oh. My. God. I'm quick to jump out of bed, and in all my naked glory, I'm practically doing the walk of shame just to touch my Chanel tweed dress suit set.

With shock still running through me, I look around the room and realize several boxes are marked "bedroom" with a Sharpie. Still naked and thinking I may be dreaming, I open two more to find clothes and shoes that were once stacked neatly in the spare bedroom I'd turned into a closet. The sun hits something just right to my left, and I spot a silver camisole that I also recognize as mine. It's laid out neatly on the end of the bed, although the covers under it are rumpled from where I tugged the covers up this morning. A note lies beside it.

For you, my wife.

I'm not sure if it's the euphoria of having a piece of what I left behind back or simply the surprise—I do love surprises—but I can't stop smiling as I slip on the silk nightie in a flash and quickly pad off to find him. My bare feet smack on the floor as I make my way and then instantly stop.

I don't understand the emotion I'm met with. Some things are still in boxes, but others are neatly placed where they should go in a home. Where they used to be in mine.

"Ro," I call out his name as I make my way through his place. His office door is shut, and I knock twice before opening it. However, I find it empty, and it seems to be the only room that doesn't contain a box or stray items of mine. "Ro?" I call out in the quiet house only to find it vacant.

So I take my time, finding a home in drawers and closets for the more important items I'm glad I wasn't forced to let go of.

Ro got all of my things for me. Not only did he get them for me but he's had help because most of my clothes are organized in the second closet. The back sitting room is jammed with furniture and boxes. It can't all stay here, but I didn't realize how much I'd miss many of the pieces. A soft blue chenille throw Aspen got me when I was sick lays across the leather wingback chair at the entrance. It doesn't match at all, but it's mine.

And it's here.

In his home.

The one that he's making room for me in.

Swallowing down the emotion, I head back to the bedroom to look for my phone.

The moment I find it, I text him.

Brooklyn: *How did you do this?*

Ronan: *You needed your dresses. I did what I had to.*

His response proves to subdue the joy and relief that's

stayed with me since I saw the clothing rack.

Brooklyn: *What do you mean?*

Before he can respond, I follow up with:

Brooklyn: *You didn't break in and steal it, right?*

My father isn't an easy man to negotiate with. In fact, I've given up even attempting to do so. As I sit on the end of the bed, I slowly realize that's exactly what Ronan did. My father wouldn't willingly allow anyone anything easily. Certainly not the man who fucked his daughter on 4k. My stomach turns in knots for a moment, thinking my father will have him arrested. Or that we'll be served a lawsuit for him stealing or whoever he ordered to go grab my stuff.

Fuck, it isn't worth all that. Just as I text out a message relaying my fears, Ro texts me first, and I delete my message entirely.

Ronan: *Don't worry about it. Get dressed and go to class.*

I don't hesitate to respond. Don't worry about it... as if I can just turn off the last twenty-some years of my life and pretend my father doesn't just get even when someone pisses him off.

Brooklyn: *I don't want you to get into trouble.*

Ronan: *Are you happy to have your things?*

Brooklyn: *Yes.*

Roman: *Then it was no trouble at all. Now be a good girl for me today and get your ass to class. I want to kiss you in something far less revealing than what you wore last night.*

Brooklyn: *Yes, Professor Wolf.*

My lips pick up in a half smirk, and that nervousness settles down just at the thought of kissing him again. Just as I'm about to toss my phone down and figure out what I'm going to wear today, my phone pings again. I expect it to be him, but it's not.

It's Aspen.

Aspen: *What are you doing?*

I can already imagine her reaction as I respond.

Brooklyn: *Going to class today.*

Aspen: *What fucking for?*

I almost answer "hell if I know," but instead, I text back.

Brooklyn: *I want to see my fiancé in action.*

Aspen: *New kink?*

I can't help but laugh. Then I start to wonder what it is exactly that I've gotten myself into with Professor Wolf. Whatever it is, I apparently can't say no to him, and I'm beginning to think...

He can't say no to me either.

CHAPTER 12

RONAN

A few days pass with ease between myself and Brook. Almost too easy.

It appears she has a fondness for gifts, even if those gifts are boxes of things she already owns. The past three days have been just like today.

When I wake up, her small frame is pressed to mine, and I have to carefully climb out of bed so I don't disturb her.

I quietly leave the apartment before she's up, allowing her to be sound asleep in my bed, looking far too innocent and at peace and like she belongs there. We share small glances in the halls of the university when I see her around one fifteen as she goes from one class to the other.

Today, she wore a sexy little tweed number I recall hanging on the rack from her place. My little whore looks like she could handle a boardroom in that dress suit. Around three, she texts me something highly inappropriate, which I'm looking forward to more and more.

Today was a snapshot down her blouse. The lingerie hugging her curves with her pouty bottom lip just barely seen in the picture.

Fuck me. I don't know how she delicately balances innocence with sex kitten, but the combo has me under a spell with this woman.

I take my phone out for another peek at the photo she sent me. I close my eyes in the empty lecture hall as I gather my things and stifle a groan as I click the briefcase shut on my desk and know she's waiting only for me.

Every day at six fifteen, which my Rolex reads is the time right now, I can finally head home, a briefcase in hand and a hard-on for her gorgeous ass.

Our routine continues.

I get home, we have a quick fuck and then takeout with small talk. We round out the night with her pretending to read from a textbook while some trashy reality TV show plays in the background. All the while, she lays next to me on the couch while I catch up on emails and, unbeknownst to her, updates from the PI and lawyers.

Just before I leave the lecture hall, I grit my teeth as

my phone goes off again. This time, it's an email from the fucking dean.

Her old man.

I check the time. 6:17 p.m. Shoving the spike of anger down, I click the email. I know it's about the emergency board meeting called by her father this morning. The one I decided to ignore.

That fucking prick.

No one knows about the bullshit between our lawyers unless her father told them this morning. He would be a fool to do so, and although I don't respect the prick, I've never thought him to be short-sighted. Other than that, though, I have no idea what the meeting could be about.

He should have known I'd issue a C&D with the bullshit he pulled over Brook. I'll fucking bury him in legal if he keeps pushing her.

Pushing me.

He should know better, given this isn't the first time he's fucked with me, and I've fucked him back.

With a deep inhale, I steady myself, still at my desk, as I read the message. By the time I get to the end of the email, an arrogant smirk graces my lips. The provost having concerns over resources of the board in response to a bullshit meeting called by her father this morning is a reprieve I wasn't expecting.

I hope that puts that prick in his place. I still have no idea what exactly he called a meeting for, but I don't give a shit. I'll be sent the notes from the secretary for it, and I suspect they'll go directly to my lawyer and only help me in possible criminal charges against the motherfucker if he did mention the legal ties we're tangled in right now. I need far more than him simply kicking his daughter out to solidify charges. However, harassment is looking more and more possible as he continues his neverending bullshit antics.

A part of me hopes he'll leave it be. He's lost. I've won. It's fucking over. But the other part of me wants him to push so I can fucking destroy him.

My oxfords smack on the polished marble floors of the university as students and other faculty walk by, and I try not to think of the bullshit. I offer a nod of acknowledgment and a semblance of a smile to those who greet me.

To say it's irritating that her father is the fucking dean is an understatement.

Her father is adding fuel to a fire that is already raging. The PI has hit dead end after dead end, and my lawyer's been hit with a slew of threats from her father's legal team about his daughter's very legal right to acquire her belongings. His threats are nothing but smoke and mirrors. He can't do shit, and if he does, he'll be wasting money.

His and mine.

My only concern is that he may have more spite than sense…and with Brooklyn getting more and more comfortable in my bed, I wonder if I also reacted too quickly.

After all, she didn't need her things the very next morning. I made a statement. One that's obvious he's heard crystal fucking clearly.

Turning left down the hall, I head out of the university building, but before I can open the door, Mr. Micheals calls out my name from down the hall.

My hand drops from the glass knob, and I turn to him. "Mr. Micheals, how are you?"

The university hall is grandeur and traditional for such an elite university. One of the hardest to get into. Bottom line, you either have the GPA, or your parents better donate a new wing to get their kid accepted. And trust me, even then, they're not guaranteed a spot in the lucrative college.

If you do make it in, you're set for life. The connections you acquire just in the four years of your attendance are relationships that will hold weight and power when finding a job or career. That's what the wealthy do for each other. Sadly, the world is hardly about what you can do. It's more about who you know.

I don't make the rules. It's just the way of this high-class life. These aren't simply students coming from middle-class homes. No, these students are born with a silver spoon in their mouths, riding to preschool in a limo with a driver.

These students wouldn't know real life if it smacked them on the ass. This is why I never wanted to depend on my old man and made my own money, which I now seem to be endlessly spoiling Brooklyn with.

If the girl can do one thing, it's spend money. It appears to be her favorite hobby.

"Doing well," Mr. Michaels replies with an exaggerated sigh, moving to hold his briefcase with the other hand. "How are you?"

"It's been a long week, but I'm happy it's almost the weekend."

"You didn't attend the meeting this morning," he states matter-of-factly, though the inflection in his tone makes it appear to be a question.

"I received the email for the emergency, and unfortunately, I couldn't attend." I lie through my fucking teeth, and I know he's a smart man. He sees right through it.

"Couldn't? Or decided not to?" he questions, cocking a brow with mild concern.

I attempt to keep my expression neutral, but the tension and irritation show no doubt because he raises a hand as if in defense.

"There are extraordinary circumstances that make certain matters and relationships delicate."

For a moment, I do wonder what her father said to him. But the moment passes quickly.

"I don't care what her father attempts to do or wants from us. If it's required, I will pursue things to the full extent of my abilities."

The professional language is at odds with my internal thoughts, but surely, I can't tell Mr. Michaels that I'll fuck her father with the iron fist of the law if he harasses or otherwise harms my wife.

Fiancée.

Fake fiancée.

Whatever they think she is to me.

I don't give a fuck.

I've known her father is a prick all my life, but I always imagined he was different with his daughter. I know better now than to give him the benefit of the doubt when it comes to anything.

Especially Brooklyn.

I add, "His disappointment with my relationship with his daughter should not be taken to board meetings. I'm sure you can agree, Dominick?" I use his first name deliberately.

"Don't make me regret supporting you in this," he says flatly, in an unfamiliar tone.

"I wouldn't," I assure him. I think he's finished, but the old man continues to pry.

"What happened between you and Brook's father?"

"I love her, and he doesn't want me with her. It's that simple," I tell him, lying to his face.

There's a history between him and me that her old man has never let on about before. Perhaps out of embarrassment.

He didn't watch the chess pieces close enough.

A business deal went south for Chambers, and I'm all too aware he figured out the details on that one. After all, I bought stocks, merged a company, and left him with a shell of what he thought he was buying. It's not the first time someone in these circles has done something similar.

It did, however, tank his ten million investment. I didn't even profit half of what he lost, but it was worth it for the sheer joy of it back in the day. Almost five years ago. There are years of my father and hers fucking one another over. It's natural when businesses compete; there can only be so many partners in deals. It was a little tit-for-tat, I suppose.

"Wasn't there something before?" Mr. Michaels questions, and I shake my head in denial.

"So it's just that you've taken to his daughter?" Mr. Michaels asks, and I nod shortly. He didn't much like me before, but the feeling was mutual and we could entertain being in the same room with each other.

"Though you are engaged?"

"Yes. Of course we are."

He nods slowly and glances down, a telltale sign of disbelief for a fraction of a moment.

"I wouldn't be with her if I didn't love her," I tell him a bit too quickly, staring into his eyes so he knows I'm telling the truth... even if I'm not. "My team is still determining the individuals responsible for the event that occurred," I add vaguely, and I'm surprised when his brow raises in shock.

"Individuals?" he questions. "As in plural?"

"It's to be determined," I answer pointedly, then glance at the door.

"I trust that you will keep me in the loop, should I be of use?"

The first bit of relief washes over me as I nod and open the door for us to exit.

"Of course. As soon as I know, you will know as well, and I'll formally address the board with your advisement."

Again, another lie.

However, I think he believes this one.

No one deserves shit from either myself or Brook. Not a single fucking one of them.

She's mine.

That's all they need to know.

Well, that and that anyone who fucks with her will deal with me from now on. Not momentarily.

But for the foreseeable future.

CHAPTER 13

BROOKLYN

My pen tap, tap, taps on the desk, and it's not until the guy next to me with a buzz cut and clean shave gives me a side-eye that I stop and sit up a bit straighter.

Calculus is boring as fuck, and I have no idea why I have to take it. I won't use it, and whatever I do with my life, I won't use letters in equations... if for some odd reason I have to, I can google it.

The professor's voice drones on, his deep timbre billowing in the large lecture auditorium. If I slip out, I'm sure he'll have no idea. There are at least sixty students in this room, and it's obvious the ones at the very front truly give a fuck.

Me and my stiletto heels that match my emerald-green

velvet jacket dress do not give a fuck... but I'm trying.

Ronan said he wants me to make him proud... so I'm here at least.

Sighing and then clearing my throat, I glance down at my notes and back up to the board. It's pretty much what I gathered from the textbook. I just don't know that I'll be able to remember all the fucking equations for the test.

Unease spreads through me at the thought of failing. I'm a damn self-fulfilling prophecy, and I know I am. Aspen's told me that more than once. I feel like I'll fail, so I don't show up, ensuring I do fail.

But what does it matter if I don't make it?

It's not like anyone ever expected that I would. It's fucking calculus. I'm sure anyone in their right mind will bet I'll finish this semester with a C or lower. I'm lost in thought, so the bell ringing catches me by surprise, and I look down to see I've only doodled "Mrs. Wolf" on the notebook for the past few minutes.

I huff a laugh, then shut the notebook and slip it into my nude carryall. I check my phone and find nothing from Aspen or Ro, but I scroll socials and see several posts about upcoming events. Instantly, I toss my phone into my purse.

I'm not ready to see any of them.

Not a single fucking one.

I need a ring on my finger before I stare down the social circles of the NYC elite. It's not lost on me that none of them have messaged me or even reached out once since the video was also emailed to their phones.

My blood runs cold, and I shake off the fucks I'm giving and stride down the hall, loving the sound of my heels. I don't need them. I don't need anyone… but I want a view of my fiancé's ass.

Even if our relationship is fake, the fucking isn't. And somehow, it's making this entire charade worth it. I do need a ring, though… maybe I should add that into the contract I still haven't signed.

I hear him before I see him. Even in the sea of students, the clacking of shoes on the hard floors, and the murmurs and chatter, his voice cuts through it all. What he's saying doesn't matter. His timbre echoes through my body.

Who would've thought him calling out that an essay was due by the end of the week would light every nerve ending in my body on fire?

Professor Wolf is hot as hell, and he's all mine.

His class ends only minutes after mine, so I wait for the students to file out. I'm almost certain he has a lunch break after this. Just as I thought, when the last student has left, he strides out of the classroom and locks the door behind him.

"Professor Wolf," I say as sultry as I can, and he turns to see me standing there, my carryall held directly in front of me with both hands. I sway just slightly, letting my dress sway along my upper thighs. It's a bit skimpy but paired with the long camel blazer that extends past the dress, it's somewhat appropriate for a daytime look.

And even if it wasn't, I don't dress for anyone but myself. I wear what I want. I always have, and I always will.

His gaze rakes down my body, and I consider slipping the jacket off now, yet I have a better idea.

"You look beautiful, my wife."

"You keep calling me that," I correct him, "It's fiancée."

He meets my smirk with one of his own before leaning closer and telling me he's just practicing.

"Is this when I kiss you?" I tease him, and his eyes drift to my lips instantly.

Kiss me, my heart begs, but he doesn't.

He glances down the hall, and I already know the answer. Wife or fiancée or whatever, making out in the hall is certainly not a good look for a teacher. Especially not with a student.

"I actually need you, Professor," I tell him matter-of-factly before he can answer. Adrenaline races through me, hoping he'll play along.

"What for?" he questions, and I turn on my heel, looking over my shoulder and requesting him to follow me.

"What are you up to, Brooklyn?" he questions.

I purr back, "You have a lunch break, don't you?"

He stays to my side as I take him up the stairs to the upper level. The clicking of my heels stops as we enter the library, and I step on the carpet in the main section. It's far less busy in the library, but there's a back room that's simply perfect. Inside, sheer delight at what's to come takes over. I've daydreamed about this moment since last week when I first saw the room. I think Aspen was right, I have a new kink.

He whispers at the shell of my ear as we walk. "What are you doing in the library?"

"I was looking up a book on stars, not that it's any of your business," I retort. I guess I can thank my astronomy class for something productive.

Grabbing his hand, I take him through the rows of shelves while the warmth turns blazing hot with each step.

"A book on stars?" he teases as I open a door to a room of classics. The title just above it is worn.

It's probably been here since the university opened, and this back room isn't carpeted like the others. It's worn wood that hasn't been updated, and the room smells of old books.

"Well, I was looking for a book, Professor, and I found this room that seems very empty … and back here …"

I check the six rows and find it vacant, then turn back to the door. A small lock is practically ancient, and Ro watches as I latch the door. I stalk back to him, and I love the way my heels sound like a tease.

"Right there, no one would see," I point, then walk past him to the shelf.

"You know, before you, I had a stellar reputation," he taunts as he stalks toward me. "I was from wealth and bred into this life," he murmurs roughly as he slips his hand up my skirt, his chest to mine. My back presses against the shelf, and I love it. He plays with my clit as he continues the nonsensical thoughts I choose to ignore in favor of pleasure.

My bottom lip drops, and I let out a small moan without consent. Yes. This is exactly my dream come true.

"Fuck me, Ro," I murmur although he only nips my neck and continues strumming my clit.

"The worst thing I ever did was choosing teaching over practicing law, which was spun to be admirable," he whispers in my ear, sending a shiver down my shoulder. "Then you showed up."

The pleasure builds far too quickly, and I have to lean against him for support. I breathe the plea with my eyes closed, "Please, Ronan."

"Please what?" His words open my eyes, and I stare deeply into his gorgeous gaze.

"Please, Professor Wolf."

He laughs at me, although he doesn't stop what he's doing. "That's not what I meant, Brooklyn."

My lust-filled head can barely focus.

"Be a good little slut, and beg me to let you come."

"You're a fucking prick," I manage, and he slows his motions, but I grab his forearm and give in to his wishes.

"Please make me come," I beg him as if I'm nothing but a fuck toy for him there in the library between the stacks of our university.

He kisses me once short yet demanding and powerful before strumming his deft fingers against my swollen nub. Pleasure rushes from the depths of me. My head falls back against the shelf as small moans escape. He attempts to stifle them by kissing me again, but I can barely stay focused on the task at hand.

"Please," I beg him again, feeling so fucking close. "Please fuck me."

I don't have to beg him twice for that one. He turns me around, and I brace myself, gripping the wooden shelf as he pulls up my skirt and enters me with a swift and forceful stroke. His hand wraps around my throat, pulling my head back, and he tells me to be quiet. His jacket and thrusts fill the room with a muffled sound and at a relentless pace.

His teeth drag down my neck at the same time his fingers find my clit again, and I come undone, barely able to keep from screaming out his name with strangled pleasure.

"That's my good little whore." He rewards me with a groan, and with two more thrusts, he comes deep inside me.

He cleans me up with his tie, then shoves it in his pocket.

"Before me, you were boring," I tell him once my breath returns. "Just an arrogant asshole with money and privilege."

"I'm still a prick, Brook," he rasps, caging me back in against the shelf. "Just a prick who's good at fucking you, and I can't seem to think logically when you're around."

l smirk at his observation. For some odd reason, it gives me a sick sense of pride that l get to him like l do.

Maybe because his presence teased me for years.

He glances up to see if there are cameras as he zips himself back into his suit pants. The waves of pleasure subside, but the warmth still lingers, and l decide to put his concerns to rest.

"l already looked, Ro." l kiss him and let the tip of my nose flick against his as l whisper, "No one will know."

My heart thumps just as l let the words leave me. That's what l thought last time…

And look where it's landed me.

Engaged to the man I've had a crush on for as long as l can remember.

CHAPTER 14

RONAN

The article a friend forwarded to me is short, deliberate, and leading.

I figured it would come, but seeing it in black and white causes anger I didn't realize I could feel.

Given the social circles are all too aware of the previous scandal, I imagine one of them planted or even sold the story to the press.

Socialite Brooklyn Chambers, heir to the Chambers mogul, and Ronan Wolf, are apparently engaged after a quiet - or not so quiet - fling. Rumors swirl about their whirlwind relationship, and given Brooklyn has been spotted without a ring, speculations on these two are running wild.

The included photo is a recent snapshot from campus just outside my classroom door. Thankfully, it's not in the fucking library. Just knowing someone photographed us on campus gives me an uneasy feeling. I couldn't give two shits about the articles and the rumors. But the fact that someone came to my work and took a photo of her with the intent of painting her in a negative light... It's violating. It could be far worse, but I wish they'd leave us the fuck alone.

All in all, it's a blip in the tabloid, but the picture... the photograph is what I can't get over.

I've been mostly careful with her over the past two weeks. Appropriate and maintaining decorum... apart from a secret fuck in a back room... twice.

How can I resist when she tempts me like she does?

When a woman like Brooklyn wants me as she does?

When she cries out my name like I'm her fucking salvation...

I swallow thickly. We need to be more careful.

I can't ruin everything I've worked my ass off for.

Sitting in my office at the university, I consider how she'll react. From the mahogany wood table to the leather couch and stacks of bookcases lining the walls with my law books, the room has an old-money aroma and atmosphere. My office is my sanctuary.

I text my friend Ace.

Ronan: *Thanks for the heads-up.*

And before I can put my phone away, he messages me about the gala next weekend.

Ace: *You attending the charity event?*

The message irks me to no fucking end. Every fucking year for as long as I can remember, I've attended as has Brook. I'm a fucking Wolf, after all. These events are among the few moments I even see my father anymore. This one, in particular, is charity-based and includes caviar and champagne.

Anyone who is anyone attends, writes a check, gets their photo taken on the red carpet for the tabloids, and rubs elbows with the other wealthy elite of New York.

I nearly write back to my lifelong friend why the fuck wouldn't I?

But I know exactly why he suspects I won't come. Public relations will recommend I lay low. Don't say anything, don't go anywhere. Don't do anything notable after a scandal.

This, though?

What's between Brook and me is not a fucking scandal. This article isn't shit. There are closed circles who saw the video, and it went nowhere. If we were engaged, it's not a fucking sin that I enjoyed her cunt on my own fucking property.

Ronan: *Of course I am.*

I write back to Ace and ask him how the West Coast is treating him and if he's returning for the event.

Ace: *I'll be there.*

He then follows up, asking when the wedding will be.

I stifle a laugh and tell him what I told the group chat two weeks ago after the video and gossip made its way through the DMs and socials.

Ronan: *We're undecided at the moment.*

Ronan: *We haven't started planning yet, but Brook might have some ideas. You should ask her at the event.*

Lie after lie after lie.

I don't fucking care at this point, though. It's like fodder for a fucking gossiping magazine.

It was entertaining when I was younger, but now?

I don't have time to check how I'm being judged. Or what they think of Brooklyn. They don't know her like I do.

The thought resonates as Brook can be heard down the hall from my office. I glance at the clock. It's past eight in the evening. Time got away from me, and I imagine she's in need of attention. Especially if she saw the article.

Fuck all of them.

I hear her heels clicking first, and by the time I glance down at my phone and look up, I'm met with a gorgeous sight.

She's wearing a colored shirt with a pleated skirt, looking every bit the part of the schoolgirl she's trying to portray. Her outfit drives me crazy. It's endlessly classic like an old movie that's a timeless piece. Her blond hair is in low pigtails, hanging down the front of her shoulders, and when her eyes meet mine, she blushes just slightly.

"Was I drooling?" I ask her, tossing down my phone and not giving a damn that it vibrates with a message as it hits my desk.

She lets out a giggle and tucks a stray hair behind her ear. "A little."

"You look beautiful tonight."

"You want to make dinner with me?"

"You're cooking?"

"Yeah, why do you look so shocked?" She feigns offense, and it's comical.

"I didn't know you knew how to use a stove."

"We could order out... or I got one of those pizza kits."

I smirk at her and debate going out. I debate being seen

together. Then my gaze falls to her ring finger. I clear my throat, wanting to get this out of the way.

"Did you see the article?" I ask.

"I did. Aspen sent it to me."

"And?"

"Is there any way your PI can figure out who took the photo?" She glances down, then back up at me. The photo got to her as well.

"More than likely not, but I've already emailed them the article, and they said they would get back to me."

"You think it was my father or someone he paid?"

I hadn't, actually.

"Perhaps," I reply, wondering why she immediately assumes it was her father.

"I was thinking it was more than likely someone who was tipped off from the magazine."

"Of all the scandals in the world, being engaged but not having a ring on isn't even on the fucking list... I think this is more like a threat," she says.

I study her expression. "Like someone saying I know it's fake... and that's what the scandal really is, you know?"

"Like your father?" I question, and she swallows thickly.

"You think he's following me? He did it to my mother."

"Maybe. You okay?" I ask her as she leans against the doorframe. I rise from my chair when she says she's fine, just that it got to her more than she thought it would. "I had my guard down at school, you know?"

I nod and make my way to her before kissing her forehead. She closes her eyes and leans into me.

Looking at her naked finger again, I ask, "What do you think about a ring?" I have a ring that would put an end to the rumors, but my heart races just thinking about it.

"I think I have a lot I could wear on this one if you want, or I have preferences if you want to drop about 50k."

I tell her easily, "Fifty K for a ring and good publicity sounds cheap if you ask me."

"I have other options as well… it's not coming out of my pay, is it?" she jokes, and I attempt a half laugh, but it falls flat.

For a moment, I forgot.

Maybe it's because it's so obviously us versus them. That will fade, though. This will pass, and then this little vixen named Brooklyn won't keep turning my world upside down.

"Oh, what time is it?" Brooklyn seems distracted.

"Why?"

She takes me to the large paned window to point out the stars. "I learned it in astronomy today." Her small hand over mine and the excitement in her tone make me think she'll be all right and this article won't keep us up tonight.

"Look," she says and points up. "The bright one is Jupiter."

"Jupiter?" I question, raising a brow.

"Did you know it's the largest planet and named after a Roman god?"

She renders me speechless.

Has my girl just found something she enjoys? I smirk at her. "I thought it was stars you were interested in?"

She shrugs. "I like both."

"Which is your favorite?"

"I'll tell you one day."

"But not now?"

"No, not now."

"Why not?" I ask.

"Because you haven't earned that part of me yet," she says seductively, teasing my tie with her polished nail. I suppress a deep groan in my chest as my cock hardens.

"And what do I have to do to get that honor?" I ask as she bites down on her bottom lip.

She purrs, "I don't know, but I'm up for suggestions."

With that, I grin and go back to answering some emails. Out of the corner of my eye, I see her reading a book on the couch by the large bay window. It's late, and no one is on campus. It's only her and me.

"Like what you see?" she baits, catching me watching her with nothing but intrigue and heat in my eyes.

"I like what's underneath."

"I'll be here, reading and waiting for you."

Unable to resist, I ask, "What are you reading?"

"A romance novel."

"Is that right?"

"Yes."

"Have you got to any of the good parts yet?"

She smirks, slightly blushing. "Maybe."

"Who would have thought my sweet little kitten would be such a dirty little girl?"

"It's romance. There's a storyline too."

"I bet. Does reading your romance novels get you wet?"

She smirks. "No."

"No? I think you're lying."

"I read it for the love story."

"Fucking can be loving."

She shakes her head, giggling. "You're so romantic."

I don't hesitate to order, "Read it to me."

CHAPTER 15

RONAN

Her eyes flicker with nothing but lust, knowing where I'm going with this. She grips her book and flips the pages until she finds what I want her to read to me.

"Are you sure?"

"Absolutely."

Her gaze intensifies for a second before she starts reading, "He slowly slid my panties down my body, making sure to leave me wanting more. Wanting everything. There's a wake of desire and lust with each stroke of his fingers running across my delicate, creamy skin."

I stand, making my way toward her, and her eyes widen, taking in my sudden change in demeanor. In five steps, I'm closing the blinds and carrying her over to my desk. When I drop to my knees in front of her, she lightly gasps as she quickly realizes what I'm doing.

I proceed to do exactly what she just read aloud. Her eyes catch mine, and she seductively smiles as I slip her panties down her legs before tossing them aside, waiting for her next direction.

"He spread my pussy open for him, watching with fascination as my face flushed from the headiness of his actions. I didn't have to speak—my body spoke for itself as he continued to look at my most sacred area with so much desire, I found it hard to breathe."

I spread her legs open for me, licking my lips in anticipation of what was to come.

Her.

All over my face.

"My arousal was evident on my parted pussy, and when he placed the palm of his hand to my throbbing nub, I let out a loud moan."

My hand slides up her thigh to her sweet pussy.

"Keep reading."

"His hand glided forward and backward on my clit, my wetness making it easy for him to do. The moisture pooling between my legs was audible with each swipe over my clit, and I almost died of embarrassment. With his other hand, he slid his two fingers into my opening, and my head fell back."

When I thrust my fingers into her warm, wet heat, she lets out the most incredible moan.

I demand, "Keep reading, or I'll stop."

There she is, spread for me. She's still wearing her outfit. All I took off were her panties.

"Ro—"

"It's Professor Wolf to you, Brooklyn. After all, you are my student."

"Am I now?" she puffs, rocking her hips in the opposite direction of my asault.

"I said to keep reading. Unless you want me to stop."

"No, Professor Wolf." She lets out an unsteady pant. "He began to finger fuck me ever so slightly while he manipulated my clit, driving me to the brink of insanity. Making me wild with need for his big, hard, thick cock."

"I like hearing the word cock come out of your sweet, little mouth." Following what she reads, I slowly move my fingers back and forth, repeatedly hitting her G-spot. "Keep reading, Miss Chambers, or I'll have no choice but to fail you on this assignment."

Playing her part like I know she will, she replies, "He did this a few more times until I couldn't take it anymore, and my back arched off the bed from the powerful release of his skilled fingers."

"Does Miss Chambers want to come?"

"Yes..."

"Should I let you?"

"Yes..."

"Why should I let you come?"

"Because I'm a good girl."

"Would a good girl be spread eagle on my desk? Begging to come like a little whore?"

"Please, Professor Wolf. I don't want to fail your class. I need an A plus, and I'll do whatever you want."

"Well, who the fuck can say no to that? But first..." I coax, leaning into her mouth while I finger fuck her, and she rides my hand. "I want to take your ass."

She freezes. "Wait, what?"

"You heard me."

Her wide eyes search my face for any sign of humor. I'm not laughing. Far from it. I'm adamant about making it happen.

She was mine to do with as I please.

Moving my fingers faster and harder, we lock eyes as she begins to come apart.

"Oh God..."

"How bad do you want an A plus, Miss Chambers?"

"So bad..."

Before she can give it too much thought, I lick from her collarbone to her breasts, sucking her nipples into my mouth.

"Fuck my hand, Brooklyn. Yeah, that's right ... just like that. Ride my fingers like you ride my cock."

Her body arches, her eyes roll to the back of her head, and her hands fist the edge of my desk. I don't let up, knowing what she loves.

Until she exclaims, "Ro!"

Her body.

Her soul.

Her heart.

It's all mine.

And I have no intention of ever giving them back.

I allow her some mercy for a moment, letting her catch her breath. Until I grasp her thighs and lay her pussy right against the edge of my desk.

I'm far from done with her. Gripping her thighs, I don't hesitate to bury my face between her legs.

Needing to taste her.

Eat her.

Fuck her with my tongue.

My rough hands seek out her breasts, kneading them and pulling at her nipples. I make her come with my mouth. Her body shakes, and her legs squeeze the hell out of my face. Still, I don't stop. Instead, I hold her down by her legs.

Sucking.

Licking.

Fucking her with my mouth until she begs for mercy.

When wetness covers her ass, I gently push my middle finger inside her ass. Her body locks up, but only for a second. My mouth becomes more urgent and demanding, sending her into a frenzy and making it easy for her ass to take my fingers.

Once she's focused on her pleasure, I begin sliding in and out of her hole. She pants in a heady tone, not expecting how good I can make her feel. I groan, watching her come so hard as I stretch her asshole as best as I can. Getting her nice and ready for me.

She's perfection.

So beautiful.

So exposed.

So devoted to me in a way I've never experienced before.

Peering up at me through dilated, hooded eyes, she watches me stroke my dick, and I jerk off harder at the mere sight of her.

Releasing her clit with a pop, I forewarn, "The next time you come for me, it's going to be from my cock in your ass."

She licks her lips, waiting.

I flip her over, bending her over my desk with her ass against my cock. I lift her schoolgirl skirt and slowly press my dick inside her asshole, causing her to gasp and suck in a breath.

"Relax," I stress, moving my fingers to her overly stimulated clit. I work her over, trying to ease her distress. "Brook, you were made for me. You know that? You're my beautiful girl."

She breathes out, and I'm almost completely inside her.

A little deeper.

A little harder.

"Fuck," I rasp, getting lost in the feel of her. "You look so beautiful with my cock in your ass."

Her body relaxes as it gets used to my size. Once her body is ready, I thrust in and out of her at a more rigorous pace.

It's seamless the way we come together.

"Oh, Professor Wolf..."

I take what I want and what she needs, and I don't hold back. I give her everything I have. Sliding in and out of her, I relish in the ecstasy that is this woman.

"You feel so fucking good, so fucking tight, so fucking right."

I never let up on thrusting into her, and when she comes, it's like nothing I've ever felt. It's explosive and sends me spiraling in what can only be described as complete surrender.

She owns me.

As much as I hate to admit it.

To her.

To myself.

Mine.

"Yes... give it to me, Brooklyn..."

When she comes that time, she takes me with her, and I spray my seed deep inside her asshole, loving the fact. Once I'm done, I lay my forehead on the back of her neck.

She's the first to break the silence. "Did I get that A plus,

Professor Wolf?"

"Miss Chambers," I inform, kissing her shoulder. "Yes, now what will you do for extra credit?"

She giggles, and it makes my dick harden again. Except this time, she playfully turns around and wraps her arms around my neck.

"I guess that depends on whether you can go another round, old man."

"Is that any way to talk to your professor?"

"No." She kisses my lips. "It's the way I talk to my fiancé."

CHAPTER 16

BROOKLYN

Day in and day out, I convince myself I don't care what anyone says or thinks about our relationship. Another two weeks have flown by, and the charity event Ronan wanted me to grab gowns for has arrived. Suddenly, I care again.

Technically, I have to care because they have to believe the lie. But whatever it is that we have right now is good enough for me, and I don't want anyone else's opinion. Except for tonight. I have to care about what they think tonight. Taking a steadying breath, I smooth out my dress and slip in my new diamond earrings.

Both of which are gifts from Ronan. He spoils me, and I freaking love it.

I thought I would grab something from my closet, but Ronan surprised me with a red gown instead. It has a low v in the front that's trimmed with lace and a high slit on the right side of the floor-length gown. Every time I take a step, you can see my silky skin peeking through.

It's sexy as all hell and slightly inappropriate, but I'm assuming that's the point. He wants us to make an entrance, and I have no problem being his arm candy for the event to shut everyone up and stop the endless rumors circulating about us.

I swear I hear a new one every day, but the one that hurts the most is when they call me a gold digger and say I'm only after Professor Wolf's money. Exactly like my mother. It's hard to deny it, given I have nothing now, thanks to my father. But they don't know that. I hate that people think I'm like her when it's the furthest thing from the truth. I've spent my entire life trying not to be anything like her.

I've wanted to have my own identity away from my parents for as long as I can remember, which makes absolutely no sense whatsoever, considering I was dependent on my father up until a few weeks ago. Nothing of what I thought my life would turn into has happened yet. Now I'm fake engaged to a man who is starting to feel like home to me.

Little by little, I'm getting more and more used to Ronan taking care of me, and in the back of my head, I know I shouldn't. Not just because it's going to end but because I could stand on my own for the first time in my life if I wanted to. The thought of that, though, compared to the thought of being with him... it keeps me up at night.

However, it's more than that. I'm starting to fall for him in ways that didn't seem possible. There's always been a connection between us, whether or not I wanted there to be. There was no avoiding it.

"Are you alright?" he asks, sipping champagne in the limo on our way to the event. I toy with the matching red silk tie that I bought him when he showed me the dress last week. Gifts are my love language... even if I'm gifting him trinkets and clothes with his own damn money. He doesn't mind. In fact, I think he enjoys that I do it.

"Yes, I'm fine." I lie, fully aware he'll call me out on it.

He proves me right, stating, "Bullshit. Now tell me the truth this time."

I drop his tie and look down at the bubbles in the flute in my hand. "There's nothing to tell, Ronan."

He narrows his eyes at me. "You look beautiful. Gorgeous, in fact. It's taking everything inside me right now not to close the divider and fuck you senseless until my cum drips out of your cunt as you step out of the limo into the event."

My eyes widen, and a new profound heat races through me. At this point, nothing should shock me when it pertains to his dirty mouth. Except I'm stunned that his dirty words know no boundaries, and that turns me on in a way I've never experienced.

"Would you like that, kitten?"

"I thought I was your little whore? New nickname for me already?"

"Are you trying to bait me?"

I grin, setting down my champagne in favor of cozying up to Ronan. "Maybe."

"In that case, I'll call you whatever I damn well please. After all, you're my wife."

He always says it to me, and it flows out of his mouth like he's been saying it forever.

I lick my lips, indeed provoking him. "How many times do I have to remind you that I'm your fake fiancée?"

He ignores my question, spewing, "If you see your father, I advise you to steer clear of him."

I can't resist asking, "Why?" Knowing again that he probably won't clue me in.

Ronan is secretive. I know he's working hard to find out who emailed our sex tape and hasn't found anyone leading to the villain. There's a theory from the PI that it's a separate person who messaged it to our friends. I told him I didn't want theories, just the name or names.

As if sensing my stress, his hand lands on my thigh, and his thumb rubs soothing circles on my exposed skin. "Don't worry about it, Brooklyn. I'm handling it."

"You always say that. Don't you think I should know the

truth about what's happening? I mean, I'm the one who's naked on that tape."

"My cock is in the video too."

I roll my eyes. "Nobody ever looks at the guy, and besides, everyone already assumed you had a big dick, so it's not a surprise that you're hung like a horse."

He lightly chuckles. "Did you think I was?"

I shrug, not giving him the satisfaction. When it comes to me, he's arrogant enough. His ego can't get any bigger if he tries.

"You little minx."

I giggle. That schoolgirl giggle just seems to come out of me. I used to laugh at those girls, and now I've become one. If I'm being honest, I wouldn't have it any other way.

Thinking back on his response about his cock on the video, I ask, "Have you watched it?"

"Of course."

"The whole thing?"

He nods in that sexy way that makes my thighs clench.

"Ask what you want, Brooklyn. I want to hear you say it."

"How many times have you watched it, Professor Wolf?"

"Enough to remember every moan you make and how it feels to fuck my fist to the vision of you taking my cock."

I blush, but it quickly fades.

"Do you want to watch it?"

I consider it for a moment. "No."

"Why not? We could watch it together. Or we can make another one for our private entertainment."

"That's a hard no right now."

He seems taken aback by my strong response. "I would rather get through the drama of our first sex tape before thinking about another." He lets out a short chuckle, then kisses my forehead. I love it when he does that. It eases the bit of stress that has come over me.

"Would you really want to make one?" I question him.

He breaks eye contact and looks down at his watch instead of answering.

"Waiting for something?"

He peers up at me through hooded eyes. "Only for you to pull your dress up for me."

Mischeviousness sparks in his gaze, and he sets down his champagne.

With that, he closes the divider, and in one strong tug, I'm straddling his lap. I let out a small squeal.

I'm quickly silenced with Ronan's mouth. His tongue slips across the seam of my lips, and I grant him entry.

He kisses me carefully, not to disturb my makeup, before his lips find my neck. All the while, his fingers slip past the lace thong and give my clit special attention. I expect him to unzip his pants, but instead, he uses his fingers. Fucking me while curving them to strum against the bundle of nerves that has me moaning his name in both agony and bliss.

As the limo slows to a stop, he commands me to ride his fingers and tells me to come. Who am I to disobey?

My pleasure rocks through me, and it's not until it's passed that I realize we're already here. Ronan sucks his fingers as I attempt to right myself.

"Can you tell?" I ask him while quickly reaching for my purse so I can check my lipstick. My heart races, and my chest is flush, but other than that, not a hair is out of place.

"You look perfect, Brook," he says. His door opens, and I wait for him to open mine.

He holds out the other hand, not the one just inside me, to help me out of the limo. And that's when my heart stops and Ronan does something I could never in a million years imagine him doing.

The second we step out of the limo, my father is standing there. It's not surprising, and I'm prepared for it. But still, I was hoping he wouldn't be right there, especially not after that.

He's one of the largest donors to this charity event, along with Ronan's father, and always stands outside to greet the other sponsors. It shows that he cares about them and the cause, when, in fact, he only gives a shit about how many millions they're donating and how likely that is to reflect their bank accounts.

To keep up appearances, my father smiles in front of the photographers and extends his hand for Ronan to shake. And what does my devastatingly handsome fiancé do? He shakes his hand with the one he just finger fucked me with.

His wicked grin is telling, although my father doesn't catch on.

Holy fuck. The balls on this man. I can't even look at my father, so I simply follow Ronan's lead. All the while, the photos snap, and I can't help but stare at him as he smiles for them and wraps his arm around me like he doesn't have a care in the world. And like he's proud of me.

After we're inside, I simply shake my head at him in astonishment, and he smirks wide, knowing precisely what I'm insinuating before he winks at me. He excuses himself to make a call he assures me will be quick and to use the restroom. No doubt to wash his hands.

I'm left alone in an otherwise quiet hall with a simple side table and intricate mirror hanging above it.

As I wait for him at the side of the restroom, a familiar group of friends slash frenemies sees me. I'm quick to smile and wave as if there isn't a thing wrong. As if I don't know they've been talking about me behind my back.

Fake hugs go all around, and I half wonder if any are genuine.

Our entire group from way back when surrounds me— Christoff, Jasper, Asher, Ivy, and Chloe. And as always, Christoff has more than just a black card burning a hole in his pocket. There's cocaine there too. I'm taken back to a few years ago as he easily and covertly brings a quick bump up to his nose and passes it onto Ivy, who then offers it to me.

I shake my head. "I'm good." I've done my fair share of extracurriculars in the past, but there's no way in hell I'm doing anything tonight with them. Cocaine—and more aptly, Christoff—has gotten me into more trouble than it's worth.

"Oh," Jasper mocks, although he doesn't take a hit either. "Has the big bad B become a good girl now that she's engaged to an almost tenured professor?"

"Hardly. My father is here."

"That's never stopped you before," Ivy chimes in. "If anything, it's always provoked you to do more." She dusts under her nose, then glances in the mirror. They're the only two who partake, and they don't push any further. Christoff does note that it's our loss, though, and Asher laughs, focusing his attention back on his phone.

Everyone is dressed to the nines. All the guys are wearing tuxes while the girls are dressed in ball gowns. The whole event is filled with people dressed like they're ready to spend a shit ton of money.

"Just don't feel like it tonight. Thanks, though," I tell them and end the discussion. I glance over my shoulder to see if Ronan is coming, but he's nowhere to be seen.

"Congrats, by the way," Ivy says. "You two look good together."

I thank her, but I'm talked over.

"Took me by surprise. Didn't know you were into older

men," Jasper jokes, and I offer him a laugh.

It's odd between us. But we've drifted apart for the last couple of years, so I'm not surprised. But I also notice them watching me, like they're trying to figure out what I'm up to, and I hope they can't see. I hate this. I hate all of it, but I play along with the small talk and listen to the gossip. A server passes by, and Jasper grabs a round of drinks for all of us.

I gratefully accept the glass as if it's a peace offering.

"Where's Aspen?" Ivy asks me, and oh, how I wish she was here.

"Is she coming tonight?" Christoff questions.

I shake my head. "She had a previous engagement."

"Engaged like you?" Ivy quirks, and again, I laugh. The back area begins to fill, and once again, I search for Ronan, but instead, I find someone else. Someone I'm shocked to see.

Chloe follows my gaze, and her hand lands on my elbow. "Did you know she'd be here?" she asks with obvious concern. Suddenly, we don't feel as if we drifted as much as I thought we had.

"No," I answer in a single breath.

"Want me to go with you?" Chloe offers, and I know she has to realize exactly what I'm feeling right now. I give her a small smile and tell her I'll be all right, but I'll send a distress signal if things go bad. Of everyone in the group, Chloe has had my back more than once. But I have to remind myself that she didn't message me. She knew and stayed away. Not only that but any one of these people could have set Ronan and I up. Instantly, my guard goes up again.

I don't trust anyone.

"I'm going to go see her," I tell Chloe, and as I stride away, Ivy calls out for me not to be a stranger.

I can't respond, though, because I'm too absorbed by the woman in the long pale blue dress. She has always loved that color. It brings out her eyes, which widen when she sees me as if she wasn't fully aware I'd be here.

"Since when did you get back?" I ask my mother, who stands in the back of a small group of women. Almost like she's trying to hide from I don't know what but probably her ex-husband. Although why would she come to this event if she was hiding from him?

The laughter and chatter dim as I stand in front of my mom, and the other women go about their own business.

She ignores my question and offers me a stiff smile.

"You look stunning, Brooklyn, but red has always been your color."

I haven't spoken to her much since they divorced, and at times, it feels like she divorced me too. Shock led me over here, but now all I feel is regret.

"Thanks."

"Did your fiancé choose that gown?"

"Oh, so you know, then?"

"Of course I know. What kind of mother would I be if I

didn't know my only child is engaged? Especially when it's to a Wolf." She smirks, and I bite my tongue to keep from telling her that I missed her call of congratulations. "Your father must be livid. Good. I'm glad. He needs to be humbled. I'm glad it came from the hand of your future husband. And what a catch you have caught, my darling. Professor Wolf is as sexy and powerful as his father."

My head tilts, wondering if my mother is drunk or high with the way she's talking. "As sexy and powerful as his father?" I question.

"You heard me right."

"I thought you hated him?" I clarify, "I thought you hated Mr. Wolf."

She cocks her head. "No, darling. Quite the contrary. I got along quite well with Mr. Wolf."

My stomach twists with the flirtation in her tone.

"Haven't you ever wondered why there's a feud to begin with?"

"What are you saying?"

"I just want what's best for you, Brooklyn," she says, placing her hand on my arm. "I'm relieved you've found someone, and I'm hopeful you're going to start a fresh new life and make your father proud or... piss him off."

She laughs and then looks up, taking a sip from her glass to scour the room.

Her hand leaves my arm, and I realize that's the first time

she's touched me in years.

I force a half smile when she looks back at me.

"Are you happy?"

"Yes." I nod, pushing down every emotion that storms through me.

"Are you in love with him?"

"Yes." I nod again.

This is a lie.

We're a facade.

It's all fake.

Then why has nothing ever felt so real?

I hate that I don't feel like I'm lying, but mostly...

I hate that I feel like a failure.

"Oh," she says like she's just come up with a brilliant idea. "We should take a picture."

"Just one moment," I tell her. "I'm going to freshen up first." Another lie. I back away with a smile that falls the moment I turn my back on her.

As I try to shake off what's just happened, I search the crowd for Ronan, wishing we could just snap a picture to prove our presence and leave.

CHAPTER 17

RONAN

As I look around the room of the event, attempting to find my Brooklyn, I'm reminded that any of these motherfuckers could be the one who emailed the video. It eats away at me as I stand there and physically can't do one damn thing about it. If life has taught me anything, it's that your worst enemies are someone you consider a friend.

For some of them, there's only one way up, and that's on the backs of the fallen they stepped on to get there. I've been stabbed in the back more times than I care to remember. I pretend I'm unfazed by so many powerful people in the same room and continue living this lie with Brooklyn even though it feels like the truth as the day flies by us and our predicament.

Before I can find her, I'm greeted by one familiar face after another. And soon, I'm standing with an old group of friends. Each one asks their own sets of questions. Congratulations are given. Small talk is had as well as updates, and all the while, I search the room for her.

"Looking for someone?" an old acquaintance among the group asks, and at that moment, I see her, and she sees me. I gesture her over and breathe out more easily.

"Not anymore," I tell him. I once again play along until Brook stands by my side.

She places her tiny, delicate hand on my chest, and my arm extends around her back as I pull her into my side.

I introduce her. "This is my wife, Brooklyn."

She simpers. "He loves to call me that."

I kiss her cheek and whisper something about how I can still taste her on my tongue before she faces them again.

"Gentlemen, so nice to see you." Her gaze moves along the faces, and I'm aware she knows most of them or has at least heard of them. Her circles differ from mine due to age, but the circles are still small among our tax bracket.

A few of them eye her up and down with the familiar predatory regards I'm used to seeing when men take her in. But in the back of my head, I can't help but wonder if they've seen the video. An anger simmers, and I grip the tumbler of whiskey in my hand a bit tighter.

"Careful now," I say lowly to Jace, the man closest to me

who has the audacity to let his gaze wander a little too low and a little too long. "She's mine." The group laughs, and so does Brook, patting my chest as if I'm only joking.

I hold Jace's gaze long enough until he breaks it and gulps down his drink.

We go back and forth with mindless chatter. And we spend the next hour socializing, watching as we work the room together like a power couple with something to prove. All I can do is endure their constant caresses on her arm and down her back.

The way they lean in a little too close when she talks to them, making sure to keep their eyes focused on hers when they really want to be eyeing her tits on full display. Their interaction isn't the only thing that bothers me, though. What captivates me the most is how she has every man in the room eating out of the palm of her hand without even trying. I want to get accustomed to how my wife works in my element.

In our world.

This is why I fight the urge to make my presence known to her and each man she encounters. I've never felt such possessiveness and jealousy as I do here at this event. I watch her every move, from her mannerisms to the way she flips her hair when she speaks, getting these men to hang on every word that leaves her mouth.

Her subtle movements of how she stands and casually

sways her body to the beat of the music from the orchestra. She never once breaks eye contact with who is speaking to her. How she casually touches their arms or chests, making sure to laugh or smile when she is supposed to like the good girl she is for me.

She's charming and seductive, yet professional. Fucking hell, I didn't realize I could fall further for her.

As I glance up in search of a server, I realize I'm not the only one captivated by her advances. Her father is too. He wears his emotions on his sleeve and shows me everything I want to see.

Does he think she'll hide? As if I would let her. She thrives like this.

I love that she's catching him off guard with how effortlessly she has the room doting on her every word, and to prove another point I can't hold back, I escort her to the dance floor.

If she's taken aback, she doesn't show it. I grip her waist and pull her close against my torso, not leaving any room between us for one second.

She lightly gasps against my lips when she feels my already hard cock between her legs.

"Professor Wolf, you're not being very discreet."

I smile charmingly, all too aware of who's watching, kissing her cheek. "I have no intention of being discreet. You're mine, and the room needs to know it."

She weighs her words as I spin her, then bring her back to me in one fluid motion. She's light on her feet, and I find myself enjoying the night.

"Do you have any idea what you do to me?"

She beams, countering, "If your dick is any indication, then I know exactly what I do to you."

I let a rough grumble of a laugh out at her remark. "So you think this is only about sex between us?"

We turn in a slow circle, and not only is she caught off guard by my words but she's also blown away by the fact I can dance.

She ignores my question. "You've been keeping secrets, Professor Wolf. Who taught you how to dance?"

Without thinking about what I'm confessing, I reply, "My mother."

"Oh."

"You didn't answer my question."

I spin her again, letting my hand linger on the swell of her back. The gentle acoustic music turns a bit more intimate, and I pull her closer, staring down into her doe eyes.

"You think you have me all figured out, don't you?" she asks, once again not answering my question about this being only about sex between us. Perhaps that's for the best.

As the number ends, I softly kiss her lips, not for show but because I want to.

Another song plays, and Brook keeps me on the dance

floor rather than returning to the sea of people. She leans into me, and we dance for a moment without much conversation, just enjoying each other.

"Tell me something," she says just before I spin her and pull her back in.

"Like what?"

"Is there anyone you find interesting here?"

"You," I answer instantly.

She huffs a laugh. "What do you find interesting about me?"

"Everything about you interests me. Is that what you needed to hear?"

She challenges, "That, among other things."

Before I can respond, the song is over, and this time, we return to the task of mingling.

When we're back to standing with my group of friends, Gerald points out, "Why have you and the dean been staring daggers at each other all night, Ronan?"

"Like you don't know," someone says to my right, but I can't break contact with Gerald, who feigns innocence.

"I mean, Ro's fucking his daughter. Of course Chambers wants him dead," James says, and the group laughs.

Gerald laughs slightly, although he looks nervously at me. "Well, maybe give your upcoming father-in-law a warmer greeting then Ronan," he says in an attempt to break up the tension.

It fails miserably.

I can be professional and civil, but I glance down at Brook, and I have no room in my heart for niceties.

"He locked Brooklyn out of her home with no access to her possessions, and my lawyers are looking into the matters of his previous divorce and the splitting of the assets. So I imagine it's more about money than him caring for once in his life about being a father."

Brook stiffens beside me for a second. This is the first time she's hearing this. I barely have time to process what's happening when my father suddenly stands beside us.

There's an immediate tension in the air all around us. The group is quiet and rather awkward. There's no greeting from him. Not that I expected there to be.

Instead, he instantly states in front of everyone, "I'm surprised I'm hearing you're engaged, Ronan." His hand lands on my shoulder. He doesn't hide the displeasure in his tone, staring only at me. Brook grabs my hand in a reassuring gesture, giving it a gentle squeeze.

"Father," I greet him as if it's not a displeasure.

The group dissipates and gives a nod in their departure. My relationship with my father is well-known to ... well, to not fucking exist.

"I need to use the powder room." Brook excuses herself, and I kiss her temple before she can run off.

As the group leaves, my father takes his place in front of me, looking me in the eye. "Why am I hearing this from everyone but you, Ronan?"

"I was waiting for her ring."

"Not your mother's ring, I hope." His words sting, and I'm grateful Brooklyn didn't overhear him.

"We're going ring shopping soon."

My father eyes me skeptically and takes a sip from the whiskey glass in his hand.

"So you're not actually engaged?" he adds. "Both of us know you were always better alone. Seeing you ... like this—"

"I asked her to marry me, and she said yes," I adamantly reassure. "Get used to the idea, Father."

Meaning every last word, I down my whiskey and leave him to wait for Brooklyn so we can get the hell out of here. We did what we came to do, and now we wait for what's next.

CHAPTER 18

BROOKLYN

Another week flies by with no new articles apart from a small mention in the Gala Times. Nothing negative and I'm grateful for that. This morning, though, I can't believe what I'm seeing in front of my eyes. There's an email from my father, and I read it from the beginning for the third time.

Brooklyn,

The fact of the matter is that you've always been a huge disappointment to me, and you marrying Professor Wolf is just another thing I can add to my neverending list. But I'm going to keep this short and sweet. I'm disowning you. You think you can cross me and get away with it by spending my hard-earned money?

Think again.

I've given you everything.

EVERYTHING.

Now, you're as dead to me as your mother.

Sincerely, Dean Chambers

It's been almost two months, and I just don't understand why he won't let this go, and why he continues this... this... I don't even know what it is. He's already cut me off financially. It's like he just wanted one more stab at hurting me.

Like what triggered this? It makes no sense.

I shouldn't be upset. I know I shouldn't. It doesn't matter. He doesn't matter. However, my mind can pretend all it wants. My heart, though...

Is broken.

Tears escape, and I can't stop them. Somewhere deep down inside, I thought he might forgive me. That we could go back to at least being father and daughter. So I could have someone.

Now, I have no one. Once this charade is over with Ronan, I'm alone. I mean, of course I still have Aspen. She truly is my best friend. And Chloe messaged me after the event and wants to meet. We do have our close group of friends, and I do care for them.

But family? I literally have no one.

And what does that mean for my trust? Oh my God, is he doing this because of the lawyers? If he does this, do I inherit nothing?

My heart races, and fear grips me like it did in that café.

It's the first time in my life I feel truly desolate. The realization that this moment—this fantasy with Ronan— can't last forever.

And then I will have no one and nothing.

I have no skills, assets, or experience. I have nothing on my résumé. I don't even have one.

I think about so many things at once that I'm bawling now. Tears I can't stop pour down my cheeks. At one point, I swear he loved me. Back when my mother and he were happy. Back when I was young and I didn't get into trouble. I was lovable to him once. There has to be some part of me that he would want to love, doesn't there?

My vision turns blurry as I stare at the screen, then push the laptop away. I grip the covers up around me and use them to wipe my eyes.

I sit on Professor Wolf's bed, in the room I decorated from floor to ceiling with his money, not mine. He's everywhere, even down to the bedding.

I can still smell him.

Feel him.

Mind.

Body.

Soul.

The door opens with a soft creak. It's like my thoughts have called him or something. I can't look him in the eyes. In a pathetic attempt to wipe my eyes and pretend I'm not crying, I cover my face. His presence is felt before his fingers press under my chin, forcing me to look up.

"What's wrong?" he instantly asks, kneeling in front of me.

"Ronan…"

"What, kitten? What happened?"

I shove my computer in his direction and haul ass to the bathroom. I don't want him to see me like this.

Not perfect.

After I splash water on my splotchy face, I take a moment to compose myself. A long moment of silence passes until I walk back into his bedroom a bit more composed. He's still there. He hasn't moved from where he was kneeling. I watch as he forwards the email to himself.

"Why did you do that?" I ask what I'm contemplating.

"Do what?"

"Forward it to yourself. What are you going to do with it?" There's a hint of panic in my tone.

"Don't worry. I just need it because something happened."

My already distraught heart drops. "What happened? Something with my dad?"

"I don't know, but ..."

"What?" I press. It's all feeling too much and too overwhelming.

"The video was leaked to the press."

My mouth drops open, and I stand there fucking frozen, unable to move an inch. If I do, it's almost as if I'll erupt into a million pieces.

"Brooklyn, did you hear me?"

My eyes widen as he adds, "It's an edited video. It's mostly focused on you, and you can't tell it's me."

He's edited out. It's just me. This was just to hurt me. Not him. All this time, I thought it was about him.

I don't listen to one more word. I pick up my phone from the bed and leave him there still on his knees for me. He doesn't stop me. Not that I expect him to. With each step I take, I feel the rest of my dignity leave me. This time, my phone pings over and over again as my hands shake uncontrollably. And I ignore them all.

CHAPTER 19

BROOKLYN

All I can think about on the drive over is, well, that makes sense. The world knows I'm a slut, and my father disowning me combined with a scandal is more than likely enough to disqualify me from my trust. I wasn't planning on showing up here. I just did. My phone hasn't stopped dinging with calls and text messages, probably a few from her. And feeling numb and with nowhere that feels safe of my own, I knock on Aspen's front door.

"Brooklyn, call me ba—" She opens the door, coming face-to-face with me while she's leaving a voicemail on my cell phone. "Oh my God! I've been blowing up your phone."

Her face drops the moment she sees me, a mix of sadness

but also relief.

I nod. "Yeah, you and everyone else."

"Are you okay?" She grabs my arm, tugging me forward and closing the door behind me.

"No," I tell her, barely holding on.

Within seconds, she has a glass of prosecco in my hand, and we're sitting out on the balcony staring at each other. She lies and says it'll be okay. She asks about Ronan, and I don't answer. "He loves you," she tells me, and my heart drops. "You two are going to get through this. I know it," she says, and I love her deeply, but hearing her say that hurts more than she could ever know.

I finally confess, "I have to tell you something."

"You can tell me anything."

I let it slip out, and I can't stop it. "It's all a lie."

She cocks her head to the side. "What's a lie?"

"You know..."

Her eyes narrow. "I don't know," she says softly, not breaking eye contact.

"I'm talking about my engagement. It's all one big charade."

She lightly gasps, surprised and taken aback. Her mouth drops open, and my friend, who I grew up sharing all of my deepest darkest secrets with, looks back at me like I betrayed her. Tears prick again, and my throat feels as if I'm going to choke, but I hold it all down.

"What?" she questions like she doesn't believe what she

just heard.

"I'm sorry I lied to you," I apologize, knowing she's hurt that I didn't tell her the truth.

"Why didn't you tell me?" she asks. "You could have told me."

"I promised Ronan I wouldn't tell anyone."

"Do you not trust me?" The hurt is evident in her tone.

"Of course I do." She abruptly stands, downing her drink in one large gulp before filling it up again.

I'm hesitant at first but find the courage to ask, "Are you mad at me?"

"Yes."

We lock eyes, and mine swell with the threat of fresh tears.

She's quick to add, "But I understand."

I nod, feeling slightly less anxious now that she's aware of the truth. Now that I can actually talk to someone I trust.

"You promise you don't hate me?"

"I could never hate you," she says, hugging me.

I can't describe the feeling going through me. Knowing that at least I can trust her and she still loves me.

When she pulls back, she asks, "And what about the video?"

"I don't know who sent it or why, but at first, it was used to try to get Ronan fired."

"What?"

"That's why we lied about it," I explain.

"Oh my God. That's why the sudden engagement." She puts the pieces together. "You were just lying so he wouldn't get in trouble for sleeping with a student?"

"Something like that. There's also a morality clause and sex in a public place is… well, it's definitely on the list of 'don't do that.'"

I take a steadying breath and continue, "But then it was sent to our friends and now leaked to the press."

"And both times, I think that was intended to hurt me, not him."

"But who would do that?" she questions, and I can see the wheels turning in her mind. She's probably compiling the long-ass list of people who either hate me, hate my father, or simply would find it entertaining to see the public fallout of a notorious socialite.

She sits back in the chair in front of me, taking another sip from her glass, and I do the same. Except I down my drink like she just did hers, and she refills it before we continue.

"Promise me you won't tell anyone."

She responds without hesitating. "I promise."

"Did you watch the video?"

"I mean… you look great. Those yoga classes really paid off. And your tits looked amazing. Seriously, you've never looked better."

If I wasn't so emotionally drained, I might actually laugh. I bury my head in my lap. "Oh God. That's not what I'm worried about."

"I know. I was just trying to reassure you. It's very '90s

celebrity sex tape of you, and look how well that turned out for them."

I shake my head. I know she's only trying to make me feel better. But all I can think is that this video will destroy my life. I start to tell her about my theory regarding my trust, but she cuts me off.

"Isn't it kind of weird that the video was cropped, and he's hardly in it? Like... it's a little weird."

My stomach sinks, and I say, "I know."

"Do you think...?" I start to ask her if she thinks Ro could have been involved in it at all, but she shuts the thought down immediately.

"Don't be so pessimistic. It's not in your nature. You need to manifest good things. Here." She grabs one of her rocks off the table. She's always been a little hippie-dippie. "Hold this."

"Aspen, your crystals aren't going to save me right now."

"Hold it anyway."

I chuckle despite myself.

I do as I'm told and hold the smooth pink crystal as hard as I can, like it will magically make this all disappear.

"How much longer does your engagement go on?"

"I'm not sure." I deeply sigh. "Ronan didn't say." I almost add that I never did see or sign the contract, but I keep that part to myself.

We stare at one another for a couple more seconds when all of a sudden, there's a knock on her door. I look down at the rock like it magically brought someone here. Please be a fairy godmother who tells me I have some rich uncle I've never heard of who passed and left everything to me.

Aspen looks up with a questioning expression.

"You expecting someone?"

She shakes her head and leaves to answer it. When she comes back, I'd be knocked on my ass if I wasn't already sitting.

"Someone's here for you."

It's only then I see who she's talking about. There in front of my eyes is the man I least expect to see. I don't even know what to think of him right now. I... I don't trust him or anything that's happening.

"I'm assuming she told you the truth?" Ronan questions, gesturing to Aspen.

"No, what?" Aspen does a shit job at lying.

His expression hardens.

"Yes, but don't worry. I won't say a word to anyone. You can trust me."

He eyes her skeptically for a moment before he glances over at me. "You okay?"

"Did you come to check on me?"

"What did you think I would do?"

"How did you know where I was?"

He lifts his phone, reminding me of the tracker he put on mine.

"You're stalking me again?"

He smirks. "I call it protection."

I pick at my nails as Aspen asks if she should leave.

"No," I answer immediately, shutting down whatever Ro was going to say.

I've never felt so nervous, and I can't even pinpoint exactly why I can't shake these overwhelming feelings.

"You're tired. Let's go home," Ro says, but I don't look up at him.

"Aspen said I can sleep here." That's my only answer for him right now because I need space. And I freaking hope that she doesn't mind I just lied... I also hope I can crash here. I don't want to go back with him. I need space.

I need to think straight, and I can't do it when he's around me. I also can't tell him that. It hurts too much to even acknowledge the thoughts in my head.

It doesn't make sense that he was edited out. It just doesn't.

In my periphery, I watch him take off his leather jacket. Glancing at Aspen, I will her to look at me, but she doesn't. She looks away like she's not sure what's best.

And fuck, I don't know either.

I've never been so lost. I've never felt this low before. Like the hits just don't stop, and I can't help the feeling that it will get worse and I'll be the only one left destroyed.

CHAPTER 20

RONAN

"I can't shake the thought that she thinks I did it," I say out loud although I don't mean to.

Gerald shrugs, and the whiskey in his tumbler jostles to the point of almost spilling over the edge and onto his shirt. Gerald's place is filled with nothing but ambience. He's single and an eternal bachelor. His place reflects that too. Everything is black or gray, with no color anywhere.

The football game from yesterday plays in the background. He vaguely watches it. Drunk as fuck in his penthouse. I imagine he'd be passed out by now if I didn't stumble in at one o'clock after Brook fell asleep at Aspen's.

She barely looked at me.

Barely spoke to me.

Refused to come back home with me.

But at least she didn't self-destruct. Aspen is a good friend, and I'm glad Brook has her in her life.

Although I overheard her canceling plans with someone in the other room. Someone she doesn't want us to know about. I thought the worst at first, but it seems Aspen has someone special in her life. Someone who's a secret too. She can keep her secrets as long as they have nothing to do with hurting Brooklyn.

Out of everyone who could have done it, there's no way it's Aspen.

While I'm lost in thought, I'm also vaguely aware I'm half a bottle deep into Gerald's collector's edition of Heaven's Door whiskey, and I don't know how I'm not passed out by this point. I think it's the spite and the desperation to figure out who the hell keeps fucking with us and why.

"I don't understand why they don't just leave us alone," I mindlessly say and then recall all the ways I've fucked over as many men as I could to get ahead. That is the way. I did what my father told me. To grow my wealth and show everyone that I will get mine. I'll come out on top.

Including when I screwed over her father. And my own when I forged my own path six years ago and went into teaching instead. Law and stocks are their game.

I got my wealth, and I left. For the past few years, I've

tried to do better, but this feels like karma showed up and decided I didn't do enough to right my wrongs. Fuck, I didn't do anything to right them.

"It's got to be him," I murmur, thinking her father won't ever let me have her too.

"Who?" Gerald turns to me, pulling his gaze away from an interception.

The dull roar of the TV is nothing compared to the pounding of my blood in my ears. I can't look him in the eyes.

"She told Aspen. She wouldn't have said shit to her if she didn't think I did it."

"Told her what?" he asks and looks at me like I'm a madman. How has he not caught on yet?

I ignore Gerald's questions, my head foggy with exhaustion and also alcohol. Texts and emails have flooded my phone, and I can't answer another fucking one.

Her father hit me with a lawsuit today, claiming I leaked the video. As if I could ever do that to her? Just the thought of a random stranger seeing her like that makes me fucking furious. "He's gotten into her head, I think... I'm going to lose her."

"Told her what and whose father? Aspen's or Brook's?"

I finally look Gerald in the eyes. Darkness rests under them, creating bags, and I glance at the clock and see it's nearly three o'clock. Two hours is too many to be rambling conspiracies because I have nothing else.

"You think her father planted a video but removed you from it?" he asks, his eyes narrowed with confusion. "He hates you, not her."

My head falls back against his sofa, and I stare at the ceiling, realizing that it doesn't make a lick of sense.

"I don't fucking know, man. The PI can't find shit but a bouncing IP address, and I don't know what the hell to do."

"I don't really understand what all is going on. Probably just some ex-friend or ex-fuck of Brook's posting revenge porn, right?" Gerald guesses, and I realize he doesn't know shit about the other half of it.

About how it's not real.

About how her father is suing, and I initially sued him for what he did to Brook.

About the board nearly firing me and the web of lies we've told.

I dragged her into my old ways. She doesn't deserve that. She wouldn't be going through this now if I'd never gone to her that morning. I would have lost any chance at tenure, but it would have never gone public. I doubt it even would have been shared among our friends. I should have stayed away. She'd be happy, off being her wild and carefree self. She wouldn't be crying her eyes out to Aspen and thinking I'd do that shit to her.

Fuck, it hurts. My father is right. I'm meant to be alone.

"I would never hurt her, but I already did and didn't know

it," I conclude to Gerald as emotions tighten my throat.

I reach for the crystal tumbler on the coffee table and throw back the rest of the amber liquor.

"Dude, what the fuck are you talking about? Did you do that? Did you send the video?" Gerald's concern is clear as he shuts off the TV and squares his shoulders to look at me.

"No. Never." I stare back at him with my what the fuck expression.

"Tell me what's going on," he urges, and against my better judgment, I do. Because I don't know what the fuck else to do, and I've already hurt her too much.

I pray this doesn't come back and bite me in the ass, fully aware that it might. But I tell him everything, and I admit I need help. I need this to stop before I lose my Brooklyn forever.

CHAPTER 21

BROOKLYN

My chest heaves with a steadying breath. I glance down at my phone, knowing Aspen will be here in a second if I need her.

I tug on the black lace blouse collar, feeling as though it's suffocating. I glance at the door to Ro's place, then down at my black skirt.

All black is for mourning, Aspen said when I left her to return here. That I know, and it's exactly how I feel. I ring the bell and wait. My heart hammers, and the little voices in the back of my mind argue and worry, not knowing what to do.

He opens the door, looking like a sex god in silk pajama pants.

No shirt means I'm met with instant heat. I wish that was enough to make it all better.

"Brook." He breathes my name like it's a prayer, and I second-guess everything.

"Did you lose your key?"

I shake my head and respond, "It didn't feel right to use it."

It's then he realizes. I see the flash of recognition in his eyes, but he's quick to play it off and opens the door wider.

"Come in," he commands.

I'm past the point of wanting him to do that.

I'm past the point of anyone else commanding me.

"I don't know that I want to."

"Why are you here, then?" he asks.

"I wanted to tell you something..." The gaze in his eyes keeps me from saying what I came here to say. Instead, I tell him something else that happened.

"I got an email from the dean on my student account." I swallow thickly, remembering how much it felt like salt in a wound.

His tone and expression harden instantly, and I grip my purse strap tighter with both hands as my palms sweat.

"Your father?"

"Yes." I part my lips.

"Forward it to me." His matter-of-fact, dominating side takes over, and for a moment, I'm swayed.

For only a moment.

"I will, but I am conceding as well. I don't want you to stop it."

"Conceding to what?" he asks in a tone that grates me.

"Their judgment that my behavior is against the student code of conduct." I can't help that my bottom lip quivers. They don't allow scandals at the university. The hits just keep on coming, but this has to be the last one. What else can they take? I don't have any dignity left, so if they try for it, they'll be sadly at a loss.

Anger flashes in his beautiful green eyes, "That is bullshit. And I'll—"

I don't even have the energy for anger anymore. "I give in, Ro. I just... if I'm not there, it might all just stop."

"No," he tells me as if he can.

As if I'll just do what he says.

He adds, "You will—"

"I will do what I want and I never wanted to go anyway." My tone is just as hard as his, and I meet his gaze evenly. "I've made my decision."

His expression softens, and he stares at me from the doorway like he's shocked and doesn't understand.

"But you love it now, don't you?" he questions.

Love.

When he uses that word, everything crumbles, including my facade that the message from my father didn't cut me to the bone.

It was one night.

One mistake.

If it even was a mistake.

Tears prick at the back of my eyes.

"Brook, kitten, don't cry."

He comes out in the hall and wraps his arms around me. He holds me like he actually cares.

I can't help it.

I'm weak for him.

I bury my head in his chest, finding the warmth I desperately need and a masculine scent I've grown addicted to.

I don't want to let this go.

Not now.

Not when I need to get lost and forget and just feel like it will all be all right, even if it's just for a moment.

He leads me inside although I'm not really conscious of it all. Only when the door shuts and the familiar warmth wraps itself around me do I realize I did what I promised myself I wouldn't.

I let myself come back through these doors.

Pulling away from him, with hands still on his chest but looking him in the eye, I say, "Promise me you didn't do this."

As I swallow and his piercing eyes seem to look through me, I know at this moment, even if I thought he was lying, I would pretend I didn't see it.

Just to survive.

If he did, I don't know how I could move on.

"I swear, I would never do that to you," he discloses, and he's so very confident in the statement.

I don't know, though.

He looks at me like he's desperate for me to believe him. Like he knows he's lying.

"Fuck, I'm going to be your husband," he adds, and I know it's because he's wondering if I came here to do what I came to do. "I would never."

"It would be an excuse, though, to end it with the board. So none of what happened would be a problem anymore," I admit my theory out loud, and his expression drops.

"I didn't do this to you, Brook." But even as he says it, it's like he doesn't believe himself. "You know I would never hurt you like this. You have to know that."

I can't say anything as I war inside my head with what to do. What's right and wrong, and if either of those choices will protect me.

I don't know. I don't know anything anymore, and as I stare back at him, the little voice whispers that I know I want him. I know somewhere deep down inside me that Ro can make it all better.

"Come here and kiss me... my wife," he tells me, and I can't help it.

It's like that single statement holds all the answers.

It starts with a kiss.

Doesn't it always?

Seemingly emotional but so quickly it turns hot. His tongue finds mine, and the spark ignites between us. His hands roam my body, and I love it. I need it.

Fuck, I didn't know how much I needed him.

My clothes come off first, but he's quick to strip himself as well. And I help him with his belt, the leather singing in the air as I pull it away. The buckle clacks on the floor, and the rest of the clothes follow, making a path to the sofa.

He lays me down, all the while kissing along my neck and collarbone, then lower, suckling my breasts. Lust and desperation make my head cloudy. My nails scratch down his scalp as he travels lower.

The moment his lips find my clit, my back arches, and I moan out his name.

He licks and sucks as his hands grip my breasts, and I swear I can feel him everywhere. With all of New York witnesses beyond those large paned windows, I come undone under him.

I cry out his name as my orgasm sensitizes every inch of my heated skin. Before I know it, his lips are on mine, his hips widen my legs, and he buries himself deep inside me, all the while kissing me as if he needs the air in my lungs.

It's far more intense than I've felt before.

Ever.

With any man, let alone the depths Ro has taken me in

bed before.

He thrusts deep and deeper, grabbing my thigh and angling me how he wants me. I can't do anything but hold on as my head spins with desire and the need for more. He fucks me so hard it nears the edge of pain. But the sweet sting and threat of agony is muted with the demanding pleasure he commands over my body each time.

Over and over, he fucks me in a way that feels like love to me. I swear it does. Even at this moment when I can barely think, I know it's true. As the thought hits me, he kisses me again, moaning my name into my mouth.

I come nearly violently as he continues his relentless pace. His groan is deep as he buries his lips in the crook of my neck. He doesn't stop as he races for his own release, pushing me higher and higher until I'm falling over the edge again.

He slams into me to the hilt, and I love the way he pulses as he finds his release. I love even more how he stares deep into my eyes and only closes them to kiss me. Passionately, wantingly, and with a deep need that my own desires echo.

My heart continues to beat wildly even after the pleasure subsides.

Even after he leaves a calming kiss on my shoulder.

Even after the cool air chills my skin in his absence as he heads to the bathroom.

I can't help but stare across the room to the bathroom light with my head spinning. I can't help the way I feel, and I can't help how this all happened.

As he climbs back into bed and the bed groans, I know two things for certain.

1.I believe him

2.I'm madly in love with him, and I'll take everything the world throws at me if only he'll love me back.

CHAPTER 22

RONAN

My father's office brings back shit memories. Like I'm a child once again who's in trouble with their old man. I assume he wants to see me over the controversy, and I'd be lying if I say I'm not a little on edge about what he'll throw at me. He's always gotten under my skin.

Especially when you're a Wolf. He probably thinks I'm ruining the family name, and I take some joy in that.

Fuck him.

He's as bad as Dean Chambers.

Which is yet another thing Brooklyn and I have in common. We both grew up with shitty fathers who always thought they knew best despite the trauma and toxicity they could be causing. It's sad when you think about it. I spent years in therapy, paying a fuckload of money for someone to tell me that I'm mad at my father.

Yeah, no shit.

With a heated tingle at the back of my neck, I feel his presence before he even walks into the room. He has a certain aura about him. Almost like he's Satan himself.

His dark hair is at odds with the stark white marble covering the back wall. His high-end office is cold and stark, just like his very presence.

And without any greeting, he takes a seat across from me at his desk, where I was made to wait, and simply orders, "End your charade with the girl, or I'll tell the board that you lied, and it will destroy your chance at tenure."

Knots twist in my stomach as I lock eyes with him and keep my expression as impassive as possible.

Charade with the girl? What exactly does he know?

It takes a minute to even register the threat. My father has done a lot of fucked-up shit to me through the years, but this one takes the whole damn cake.

I don't back down, and I'm insulted that he thinks I will.

"What fucking charade? You don't get to—"

"Gerald told me everything."

Swallowing thickly, I register the hell I'm in. I can't speak. I can't say a word. What the fuck? No fucking way. Gerald?

"He had good intentions. Wanted me to help, so I am."

My father's smile twists the knife in my heart.

Gerald.

Fuck, man. I can barely breathe with the lump that grows in my throat.

He doesn't understand. His parents want the best for him. Mine wants what he feels I took from him.

I don't even flinch, scoffing out a chuckle, and immediately play it off.

"What makes you think he's telling you the truth?"

My father rebuts with another question. "What need would he have to lie to me?"

My thumb taps on the hardwood. Of everything I expected, it wasn't a threat about tenure. It wasn't that he knew we were lying. Every possible outcome races through my mind, fighting to be heard.

I respond to my father a little slower than I'd like but calmly and confidently. "I don't know why he felt the need to lie to you, but if he continues, I have no problem suing him for slander. Just how far do you want to take this?"

"As far as needed. You won't marry her. I'll destroy you both before I allow her to have my last name or a cent of Wolf money."

My hands twist on the leather armrests of the wingback chair. My palms are sweaty. It's why I should have never told him. I should have kept my mouth shut. The moment a lie slips, it spreads like wildfire.

"So end it. Or I'll end it all for you," my father says in my silence.

Who the hell does he think he is?

Instead of just thinking it, I spew in a menacing tone, "Who the fuck do you think you are?"

He holds his hands out in front of him on his desk with a cocky grin, simply stating, "Currently, I'm the man who holds your future in his hands. You can call me your god."

"Fuck you."

He snarls, "Watch it, Ronan. I'm still your father."

"In what sense of the word have you ever been my father?"

He slams his fist on the table, but it doesn't faze me in the least. It takes everything just to sit here and not react.

"I've given you everything for you to lead the life you do."

"Let's get something straight," I threaten. "You haven't given me shit. Everything I have, I've worked my ass off for."

"Oh," he mocks in a condescending tone. "You think my last name didn't get you there to begin with?"

"Stop blowing smoke. You're the only one who believes the lies you tell, you narcissistic son of a bitch. You went out of your way to make every step harder for me. You couldn't handle your son doing better than you, could you?" Somewhere in the back of my mind, I know I have a leg up, but so does he. Fuck him for thinking he can hold it over my head as if he wasn't dealt the same damn deck of cards.

"The apple doesn't fall far from the tree. I mean, look at

you. You're the spitting image of me. Except I'm more of a man than you'll ever be, and don't you forget that."

"I can't remember something that doesn't mean shit to me."

"Enough!"

"But why?" I smile and shrug. "Here I thought we were just bonding."

"Do as I say, or I'll be forced to use my hand in this bullshit engagement you pulled to save your ass from fucking the dean's daughter on your bar."

Anger fumes and rages inside me, but I stay seated. I can't even begin to think of how to fix this. Voices scream in the back of my mind, one voice louder than the others. The one who thinks of Brook and how fucked all of this is.

She never deserved any of this. I started it. I brought my problems to her, and now my own father will add to her pain. There are no depths to how low he'll go. And she's holding on by a thread.

It's then that it dawns on me.

"It's you, isn't it? You're the one who sent the email to the board?" My knuckles turn white as I grip the armrest tighter with the thought. "Were you watching the bar? Looking for something to shut it down, and instead, you found us?"

"You think I'd risk my family's name? You think I'd film you fucking like a pervert?"

I shrug. "I wouldn't put it past you."

His eyes narrow in anger like I haven't seen in years. "End

it," he pushes again, but there's no way in hell.

"You have no proof," I answer, and before I can even add my next thought, he slams a paper down.

I recognize it immediately.

The contract.

My blood runs cold. "There are no signatures."

"There are emails, though."

Adrenaline races through my veins. "And how the hell would you have access to those emails?"

"An accidental reply from your lawyer. I suppose having similar emails with the same last name can lead to accidents."

"I'll sue the fuck out of you and that dipshit lawyer." I've never felt such betrayal.

"You can do that while you're unemployed."

My hands fist, as I'm backed into a corner. In the back of my mind, I try to remember what I even wrote in those fucking emails. They're confidential, and I could sue the hell out of the firm. But that doesn't fix shit. It doesn't save my tenure, and it doesn't save Brooklyn and the backlash that will pile on top of her while she's so fragile as it is. Just more lawyers, more money being burned, and for what? For them to drag out her pain.

"Why are you doing this?" I narrow my eyes, barely containing my emotions.

"You're not going to marry her and lose all that money to a gold digger."

"She's not a gold digger—"

"What's the contract for, then?" he asks, and I don't answer. I have no more lies on the tip of my tongue.

"With this fucking video being leaked, you should be thanking me. A prestigious professor shouldn't be associated with ... that," he says the word as if she's a thing. As if she's disgusting.

"With that? She's going to be my wife." I grit my teeth, and I can't help myself.

In a single movement, I'm up from my chair, my fist curled, and I smash it against his face. My body shakes with adrenaline, and every muscle stays coiled within me. The sudden impact lands right on his jaw. His chair flies back, and he ends up on his ass. At first, I don't even realize what's happened.

I stand, chest heaving as my vision blurs. As I steady somewhat, my hand still balled, my knuckle cracked with blood, he rises.

Wiping away a bit of blood from his lip, he takes his seat as if it didn't affect him.

"Leave her alone. She has nothing to do with us."

He huffs a laugh and flexes his jaw as he pulls his seat back into place.

"Then she better prepare for you to be unemployed, caught up in legal and spending hundreds of thousands on lawsuits, oh, and possibly in jail for fraud, given the shit you pulled when you cashed out and left Wall Street."

"You don't have proof of shit," I sneer. "If you did, you would have already fucked me over." Even as I respond, I doubt myself.

I wasn't always on the up-and-up when it came to Wall Street. Thus the falling out with Brook's father. One of many examples. There's no way he could prove a damn thing, though. I'd already be in jail if he could. I know that much about my father.

"I have regrets, but I've done everything I can to make things right."

"Is that an admission?" my father asks, and it's then I wonder if he's recording our whole damn conversation. Nothing is safe or sacred, and everything swarms in my head to get the hell out.

"If you don't leave her, I won't just stop at you. I'll go after that little slut too." Before I rip his fucking head off, I get the hell out. Storming from his office, I walk into a nightmare I didn't know could exist.

And I'll be taking Brooklyn right along with me. I know with certainty that it's all my fault, and if she thought what happened before was bad, I don't know how she'll survive what's ahead.

CHAPTER 23

BROOKLYN

After last night, everything feels different. It feels real and raw and safe. For the first time in my life. I have to suppress a laugh as I realize I'm sitting in a freaking lecture and feeling grateful for being here. Astronomy class is interesting. I lean back in my seat, actually enjoying it. I know it goes against what the dean, my father, demands, but Ro told me to. He says it's okay and no one can force me out of the university. He doesn't want me to back down. I haven't done anything wrong, and I believe him.

At this point, believing him is all I have left. I'm going to bury myself in schoolwork until I can bury my head in his chest.

The clock ticks on, and class is dismissed before I'm ready.

I gather my things, realizing last night is the first time I've really slept in days. Maybe that's why I'm so … different today.

As I'm walking out of the lecture hall, I hear someone from behind shout, "Aren't you the student who's banging that hot Professor Wolf?"

Heat and slight anger run through me. The fucking audacity.

I turn to face him and just look at them until they get the hint and keep walking. A death stare will go a long way. It's been like this for days. Everywhere on campus, people look at me. It's hard to comprehend that everyone on campus has seen me naked. And if that isn't bad enough, they've seen me getting railed.

I hate that they probably think Professor Wolf might be looking like a fool for being engaged to me. He tells me not to worry about it, that he doesn't care that they may think that. He doesn't give a shit about what people say or think about him.

I wish I could be as strong as him, but the truth is, I'm far from it. I'm faced with so many things I didn't consider when we started this lie. I want to tell people the truth, but that won't clear my name. It will only make me look worse.

It's like I'm damned if I do, and I'm damned if I don't.

I can't win either way.

I focus on getting to my next class, trying to act like I don't feel everyone's eyes on me. Finally, I sit in the same seat I have since the first day of class. Way in the back where no one can see me or find me, for that matter. I'm not here for anyone's fucking entertainment, and I don't owe anyone a damn thing.

I pull out my notebook and start doodling Mrs. Wolf onto the blank pages, and for some reason I don't want to consider, it makes me happy for a fleeting moment. I get lost in my fantasy world that at the end of all this, Professor Wolf and I will be together.

I'm in love with him.

Head over heels.

Madly in love with him.

And some part of me knows he's aware of it although he hasn't called me out on it. I don't know if that makes things better or worse. Either thought makes me anxious, and I'm back to square one again.

Do I tell him that I love him?

What good will that do?

Will it make things more complicated than they already are between us?

Who the hell knows. I know he has that meeting with his father today, and I hope it goes better than he anticipates. I hope everything just gets better from here. We've been through enough, haven't we?

Question after question tears through my mind with no end in sight. The more I doodle Mrs. Wolf, the more I realize I truly am in denial of my current reality. It's insane how much your life can change in a matter of a few weeks.

I feel on edge, and that's not good for a girl like me.

I'm worried he'll think it's only about his money when that can't be further from the truth. Especially with what's going on with my trust. However, it doesn't stop the reckless thought that he'll think I'm a gold digger. Exactly like my mother.

I love Ronan Wolf.

I've never felt more protected.

Adored.

Safe.

He makes me feel like I'm not as fucked up as everyone claims I am. That I'm not just a socialite with no intelligence or skills. I've played into the narrative for years, relying on it to keep myself from getting hurt. It's so easy for me to fall into that character.

Now, I may not know who I truly am, but I know who I want to be.

And the undeniable truth is...

I want to be Mrs. Wolf more than anything.

CHAPTER 24

RONAN

I haven't been able to fucking think straight. All I know is that she needs out of it before things get worse. I never should have asked her to do this. It's my fault. Every fucking bit of it, and I'm the only one who should pay the price.

If I can do one last thing for her, it's to give her a way out. I stand as I hear her heels clicking down the hall, back home from class. Just like I've gotten used to, but today I can't stand it. Time's moved too fast.

I'm sick to my stomach when Brook comes inside my office. I back away from her, needing some space.

Her face pales. "What's wrong?"

I do what I have to do.

I do what is supposed to be right but feels so fucking wrong.

Instead of breaking it to her easily, I flat-out spew, "We knew this wasn't going to last."

She doesn't say a word, though the light in her eyes dims. It's like watching her walls go up. A version of her I used to know looks back at me, and I already hate it. I wish I could go back, but I have to do this. I've already started it. She can't go through this shit with me.

The total silence is deafening. My heart pounds, and I wait, but she says nothing. My head spins, and I lean against my desk. My knuckle is still split, and I stare at it rather than her as I tell her, "It's been over a month, and we did our part. It's a mess as it is, and it's best if we just split and lay low."

Still, she doesn't speak.

She doesn't move either.

She's sort of just there. Giving me nothing. Not fighting. Not objecting. Just there.

I can't read her one way or the other, and for the first time, it scares me. How much I can truly hurt her even though I'm trying to save her.

Love her.

"It makes sense if we split because of the scandal. I know I said it didn't matter what people thought... I was wrong."

I can't tell her the truth. I can't bring her into this.

The words feel like I'm literally spitting out battery acid.

They burn coming out, and I barely think I'll make it out of here alive. I'm going to bury us both.

I stare up at her. She's beautiful and stoic without an emotion whatsoever. I stand straighter, attempting to be the man she needs but wishing I could be selfish. Wishing I could take her and run from it all.

"You'll get the money I promised you. You can stay here, and I can move into one of my other homes. Or we can stay together... Just not. You can take all the time you need." I swallow down the harsh reality.

She still hasn't said one fucking thing, and I'm beginning to worry it was all in my head, and she doesn't feel the love for me I think she does.

Maybe I've imagined it?

Want it to be true?

She doesn't offer an option. She doesn't say it wasn't fake for her. She doesn't ask anything of me at all.

Right when I think I'll get a response from her, she spins to leave without saying one damn thing. I'm in front of her, blocking her exit before she can take a step to go.

I grip her oversized cashmere sweater and hold her close. Her leather leggings press against my skin.

It's almost like she knows I'm full of shit, and I don't want to lose her. That I'm just ending this because I have to, not because I want to.

The first thing she says to me after everything I just shared with her is, "You'll get out of my way, or I'll call the police." My body turns to ice. She doesn't even look at me.

"Brook—"

"Get the fuck out of my way." I've never heard such venom from her. It shocks me to my core.

I'm fully aware if I touch her, this will be the end of us.

It's like she wants us to end too, and it's too hard of a pill to swallow.

Why isn't she fighting for us?

It's a selfish request, thinking she'll fight me on this. It kills me that she's not. That she's just surrendering to me as if I never mattered. As if we never mattered.

I let the devil on my shoulder win.

I can't let her go.

I try to kiss her, but she pushes me away, warning in a heated tone, "Get the fuck away from me."

"You have nothing to say? You're just going to leave?" I ask her, needing to hear the truth.

For once and for all.

Some fucking truth.

No more games.

Lies.

Charade.

I need something.

Anything.

I just want her honesty. It's all I've ever wanted and never received from her. She has this wall that's built to the fucking moon, and I've done everything to knock it down. It's useless. Almost like she knew this moment would eventually come, and she's tried to protect herself from it.

I hate that I'm the man who made her think she's safe, and now I'm stripping it away so easily.

I hate that she may hate me after this.

But mostly, I hate...

That I'm so fucking in love with her it terrifies me to the depths of my core. To the bottom of my being. She's everything to me, and I can't hide from that anymore.

If she lets me love her, I will destroy her. I know it. Yet...

In a cool, detached voice, she states, "There is nothing left to say. It's done. We're done." Only then does she look me in the eyes. "It was never real, right?"

I'm once again sick to my stomach, feeling like I could heave at any second, but I suppress it all.

I tell her the truth. "I didn't want this to happen."

I want to tell her the whole truth and nothing but the truth. I'm only doing this because if I don't, my father will destroy not just me but her too. She doesn't know the hell that would come. She doesn't deserve that. She's never deserved any of this.

I want to tell her how important she is to me.

How much I love her.

Want to hold her.

I do none of those things.

I watch her leave instead.

For a moment, I think she's going to come right back. I just stand there frozen in place, glued to the damn floor beneath me.

One minute.

Three.

Five.

Until I can't take it anymore. I grab my phone from my back pocket and text her.

Ronan: *I'm sorry. Come back to me. Please.*

I hate that I sound weak, but love makes you do funny things. Never did I understand that statement until this very second.

Ronan: *We can talk about it. Something happened.*

She doesn't respond.

Not after an hour.

Or two.

Or five.

And when I'm sitting there all alone in my bedroom, surrounded in her scent, her decor, and the things from her place, the memories in this bed, I can't take it anymore and punch a wall with my fist.

"Fuck!" I scream from deep within my chest.

I hate my father.

I hate my life.

I hate the lies that have all added up. One right after the other. I have nothing left. Not my family. Not my wife. Not my world. All I'm left with is empty answers.

With my knuckles bleeding, I throw my cell phone across the room next. I know this is the end...

Of the life I wanted so desperately with her.

CHAPTER 25

BROOKLYN

Maybe some people are meant to just be alone. Like there's something wrong with the way they love. That's the conclusion I came to at Aspen's place, where I've stayed the past few nights.

I adjust the jacket slightly so it doesn't look quite as tight. Aspen's a size smaller than me, and I don't have anything else to wear. I'm not going back to Ronan's.

I'd absolutely lose it if I did.

I think I'd beg him to love me if I ever saw him again, and I'll never forgive myself if I do that.

I've loved my father for as long as I can remember. He was my hero growing up. All those memories came back to me over the past few days. My mother called me her mini me and loved me too.

We were happy once.

What happened?

I know they loved me back then. When I was just a kid and when they loved each other. Then everything changed, and at some point, however, that love just wasn't enough.

My mother hasn't said she loves me since I decided to stay with my father, and my father certainly doesn't love the person I've become.

And now Ro.

I love him more than I've loved anyone. I've never felt so utterly and completely destroyed.

So ... hopeless.

Like I'm just not meant for this life.

"Mr. Stagert will see you now," the secretary says from her desk in the waiting room.

My financial manager has always had impeccable decor. It's all clean, modern, and minimalist, but the pieces reek of wealth. As my heels click in beat with my heart and I follow the secretary down the hall, I realize I couldn't afford a single piece right now.

Maybe if Ro sends me that million, although we never signed that contract. At this point, I don't think he will give me a cent. I don't trust anything he says anymore and haven't answered a single message from him.

Instead, I've blocked him.

Seeing his name is just too much.

Texts and emails have piled up, and I've simply ignored them as well. Professor Montgomery from my astrology class has noticed my absence. An email like that, one that should have never bothered me, made me bawl my eyes out this morning.

I'm obviously unwell, so I'm just going into hiding.

Unfortunately, as Aspen pointed out, I need to face my financial situation to determine my options. Just so I know.

I need to grow the hell up.

With a deep breath, I shake the old man's hand. He's known me for as long as I can remember, but it's never felt like this. He offers me a sad smile that seems forced, and behind his thin-rimmed glasses, he narrows his eyes as he looks at me.

He unbuttons his gray suit jacket and motions to the wingback chair to the left across from his desk. "Have a seat."

With a thud in my chest and a sinking feeling, I lower myself to the chair.

"Mr. Stagert, how are you?" I ask. He tells me he's doing well and doesn't ask me in return.

I get the feeling my father has filled him in.

Fuck.

I clutch my purse and regret not getting my things from Ro. I could have at least sold them.

"Miss Chambers, I'm glad you came in because there's something I really need to discuss with you," he starts, and my throat closes up with emotion.

I second-guess coming altogether. I can't take more bad news.

"It's not wise to let the recent deposit sit. We should invest a good chunk of it, and I have a plan if you have time to look it over." He speaks matter-of-factly, and it takes me a moment to comprehend what he's said.

"What?" I barely get the word out.

"You're young, and I realize you have income now, but we need to look at your retirement, what you'll need in the far-off future." He squares his shoulders, lacing his fingers together in front of him, seeming to contemplate his next statement. He's delicate with it. "I realize there have been some changes for you recently, and I think it's best to use this deposit to prepare for life ahead. Just in case."

"What deposit?"

"From Mr. Wolf. For ten million."

My bottom lip drops open as I'm struck with shock.

Ten million.

I could cry on the spot for several reasons. But the first that hits me betrays the wall I've been trying to sustain around my heart. If he's sent me money, he's done with me for good. I'm taken care of like he promised he would. But that comes with a price.

It's a clusterfuck of mixed emotions, and I can't process things fast enough. I'm torn up from the inside out. It's not one million like we agreed on with no contract. All I had was his word. And now, his word has become ten million dollars.

How did I get so unlucky and lucky at the same time? I lost the love of my life, but I gained ten million dollars. The crazy thing is that I'd give up that money just to be with him.

And that's the God's honest truth.

There's no reason for me to deny it to myself. All I'm left with are my thoughts. Whether they're good or bad, they're mine. I can't stop the emotions as they spread over me, and the financial adviser appears quite out of place as he passes me a box of tissues.

I take one and then another, trying to control myself. I was only with him for a little over a month, yet my entire world has changed because of him.

From the moment I kissed him, everything fucking spiraled.

"I just need a minute," I tell him, and he quickly gets up, telling me he will return in just a moment.

The second the door closes, I sob.

And I can't make it stop.

I don't want his money.

I want him to love me.

It's never been more clear to me that he's all I want.

I thought it was a crush when I was younger.

I thought it was lust that night at the bar.

If it's not true love, then I don't know what it is, but I don't think I'll survive this. I don't know how I can live knowing I feel this deep, aching love for him, and he doesn't feel it for me.

I'm alone.

And in the end, it's what fate wanted for me. It's what I deserve.

CHAPTER 26

RONAN

"Destroy them all. Every fucking one of them."

My eyes are bloodshot, and I'm sure I must look like a madman to my legal team on the Zoom call. I stare at the screen, my thumb tapping in a menacing rhythm. "I want criminal and civil charges. Every fucking little thing we can nail them on."

I gave them the lead based on a hunch, and what those assholes did unraveled within hours.

Four sets of eyes look back at me, and no one says a damn word. I glance down at the PI's report, and once again, I'm shaking. It came in only twenty minutes ago, so my team has barely had time to adjust to what the fuck is happening.

"There will be a conflict of interest with my firm as we represent your father as well," the youngest of them pipes up. His black-framed glasses and clean-cut look do him no favors at this moment.

"Yes, I imagine you need to discuss it with your partners and that you'll drop him as a client, given the extent of this discovery." They better fucking drop him. "Especially given the slipup that caused him to blackmail me."

"Has any of this been verified?" Mr. Walker, the most seasoned lawyer and my longtime attorney who knows every fucking thing I've ever done, questions. "All the IPs. All the timestamps, all the—"

"Yes. He's sending it all in a zip drive. All the evidence is there."

"It's just—" Another attorney starts, and I cut him off as well.

"Hard to believe?" I question, barely holding on to my sanity. "That my father wanted to fuck me over and that hers wanted to fuck her over even more?"

They're silent as my spiteful words strike them. Not a single one answers, no doubt realizing just how on edge I am.

"What they did is illegal. What they did will have consequences. Do you understand me?"

"Is there anything you think we should know on your end?" Mr. Walker questions carefully, and I'm not sure what he means.

"Like what?"

"Any unclean hands?" he asks, and it dawns on me what he's asking.

"I didn't play a part in it at all, but I did lie to the board. We weren't engaged. It's not illegal, but I am well aware that taking this to court could lead to a deposition that will end with my resignation from the university."

"Is that worth pursuing?" Mr. Walker asks, a man of logic and only logic. He adds, "Monetarily, neither of you suffered in a way that can be directly linked to their actions. Criminally, there will be depositions, and they will be public."

"We can try to conceal them—" one attorney offers, but Mr. Walker quickly interjects.

"The likelihood of that is practically nonexistent."

"I understand my testimony will not represent me well to the board," I tell them.

I already know, and I don't give a flying fuck.

"The result may be a sentencing of a couple of years—possibly but unlikely—for your father and hers. A few thousand in fines and they'll certainly fight to keep the charges private."

"Nonconsensual dispersal of pornography is a gross misdemeanor, Ronan. You know as well as I do that there will be little to no consequences," he adds.

"Legally, I am aware. But her father will be forced to resign in the process."

"As will you," Mr. Walker reminds me. "It may not be

advisable to take a legal route with this."

The lawyer in me knows exactly what they're saying. If I pursue it civilly, I'll spend hundreds of thousands to get nothing but a public shaming of the two of them while also putting a spotlight on what actually happened. Furthing the public shame Brooklyn's been receiving. I may not even be able to file charges against her father, given the version he shared edited my likeness out.

The law is as crooked as the government. They go hand in hand. You have to be rich enough to enforce it or rich enough to fight it, but either way, laws aren't made to keep the wealthy in line.

"The two of them will likely see no real consequence, is what we're saying."

"It will be more about the public backlash for you?" Mr. Walker assumes.

"It's more about doing what's right for Brook," I tell them, and I'm hit with the devil's advocate responses I should have guessed were coming.

"Is it going to be healthy for her? To drag this out publicly?" Mr. Walker questions.

"And what will it look like for you and your reputation? Especially given you've separated," another lawyer adds.

"I pay you money, and you do what I ask," I tell them with finality as my emotions get the best of me.

"Sleep on this, Ronan. Talk to Brook," Mr. Walker advises.

"She won't answer me," I confess to them, then wish I hadn't. Fuck!

It's quiet for a moment, and I steady myself before telling them I want them to start the paperwork. I will confer with Brooklynn and get back to them on Monday.

"In the meantime, I expect you all will come up with an alternative solution?" I inquire.

The four men nod, each doing a piss-poor job of maintaining a professional expression. Concern is etched into their faces.

I hang up the call without saying goodbye and check my phone again.

None of my messages are being read, so I email her again to call me. That's it.

Just, "Call me."

Thankfully, the email hasn't bounced, so she hasn't blocked me there yet. I run my hand down my face, hating how I let her go.

What the fuck was I even thinking?

I wanted to protect her.

I wanted to protect myself.

I basically lost for us both.

If I could go back, before I ended it, I would ask her if even a sliver of it was real for her.

I know it had to be.

It was for me.

I acted out of fear even though I knew what I was doing wasn't right.

With that in mind, I look at the email I drafted while I waited for my lawyers to get on the call.

I almost don't do it because I know my head is spinning. I almost resist, but I can't.

It's the right thing to do.

I read over the email one more time, and I send it to an advocate, my friend Mr. Michaels.

Along with my resignation and apology.

I tell him everything and attach the zip drive. I don't give a fuck about the board or my job or my reputation. I have so much fucking money they could fire me and destroy my name, and it won't make a lick of difference in my life or my finances. I don't care about anything other than Brook.

When she finds out my father leaked the video first to destroy me and hers did it second to destroy her, I know it'll wreck her. My poor Brook. She's not as heartless as I am.

The moment my father mentioned the emails with the contract, I knew something was off. It wasn't an accident that he received a random email with the contract Brook never even signed. He had me followed and had been searching for something to get on me. Just to control me and get me back in line.

He never could have known Brook would be there. She was a bystander in my father's game. I told the PI to look into my father's emails, and first they found the emails to the man he hired to stalk Brooklyn, and then the threads came undone. The calls between my father and her father. The timing was just too perfect.

All for what? Money and greed?

I just wish she'd answer me.

I wish she'd let me be there for her.

I email her again out of pure, utter desperation. She needs to know what happened. I'm hoping the ten million will at least earn me a message. Anything at all. She needs the money, and realistically, it's what I stole from her father. So in some ways, it rights a wrong. But I'm hoping she will message even to just tell me to fuck off and leave her alone. I will take anything. Even if it's a slap in the face. Hell, I deserve it.

She's never deserved any of this.

Ronan: *I'm sorry I couldn't stop any of this or fix any of it, but I need you to know I am sorry... I love you, Brook. Please let me make this right and love you the way I should have from the start.*

I've said I love you to her before in front of people. This is the first time I'm saying it on my own.

And I fucking hate it's through an email and not face-to-face like I want to or like how she deserves. This time, the email bounces, and for the first time in years, I fucking lose it. Tears stream down my face while I shove my weight into the computer and knock it off the desk, screaming out in agony.

My chest heaves as I wreck my office, throwing everything I can and hating my life.

Hating who I am and what I've done.

And not knowing where to go from here.

CHAPTER 27

BROOKLYN

Day number four of going to class even though the dean supposedly expelled me. Fuck him. If I want to go, I'm going. There was no other formal email, and I don't know if Ro could do anything at all. But security hasn't escorted me out, so I assume it may have just been my father being an absolute piece of shit. Attempting to twist the knife and take away the one place I have to escape the real world and live in the stars for a moment.

As the professor for calculus drones on about an open notes test, I glance down at my emails. Several are from a lawyer I recognize the name of, I think my father's. I don't open them. Maybe I'll be served in class with some bullshit.

They do that. My father especially. Filing lawsuits just to fuck someone over. Maybe that's why he hasn't had security come and escort me out yet. He wants to make a splash with his next move.

Funnily enough, I just don't care.

The bell rings before I'm ready to leave. And I know what's next. Walking by his class. Having to rush so I don't see him. Feeling his presence and knowing I can't be close to him.

It's torture.

This moment is the part I hate the most. The reminder of what once was and how much I miss it.

How much I miss him.

My ballet flats are quiet as I walk. I barely even breathe as I get close. My grip on the small leather backpack tightens, but just as I prepare myself, I realize today is not the same.

The door is closed, not open. The light is off.

He's not here.

Curiosity gets the best of me, and I take a few hesitant steps forward, peering through the window.

Something ticks inside me. Like a hollow clock.

As I'm peeking in, a gentleman behind me clears his throat. I'm completely caught off guard, and the shock nearly stops my heart.

"Sorry," I apologize as the old man watches me.

"And you are?" he questions.

"I was just looking for Mr. Wolf."

He nods slowly, looking at me as if he knows me. It dawns on me that he might. Perhaps I should be scared or skeptical, but instead, curiosity begs me to ask what I know I shouldn't.

"What happened to Professor Wolf?"

"Nothing as of this moment."

"What does that mean?" My question comes out defensive.

"Miss Chambers, I believe?" he interrogates, and immediately, my guard goes up.

"And who are you?" I ask.

"Mr. Michaels, a friend of your ... what would you prefer I call him? Fiancé?"

It's then I vaguely recognize him from parties my father has thrown over the years.

"You're on the board?" I question, and the man nods.

"You didn't answer about Ronan," he reminds me, and I say nothing. Half of me wants to about-face and leave him with nothing. The other half begs to know why Ro isn't here and questions if this man has the answer.

"Would you like to have a private conversation?" he adds and gestures to follow him into the classroom as he unlocks the door.

"What about?" I raise my voice and harden my stance.

At this point, I trust no one, but still, an air about him begs my intuition to listen. Maybe it's because he's older and his eyes are kind. Maybe it's because he has a key to the classroom.

I don't know.

But I just can't trust it.

I can't trust anything anymore.

He only looks at me, unlocking the door and holding it open for me to follow. I only hesitate a moment before I acquiesce.

He flicks on the lights, and I follow him down the stairs. Johnathan pulls out a laptop.

"Are you teaching his class?"

"I'm not," he answers. "I happen to have a key and thought privacy would be better."

He hovers over his computer for a moment, slipping on thin-rimmed glasses. "I've known Ronan for quite a long time, and recently, he's been different."

My heart sinks. "Different how?" I remember the library, how Ro pointed out how much of a bad influence I am. I know it. I've always been that person. Someone who brings people lower.

As the older man looks at me, his lips thin into a straight line.

"Different like he cared more about something other than work. Other than his reputation."

I swallow the emotions that threaten to spill from my lips. Every single word is kept from coming out.

He doesn't care about me.

I don't say it.

I can't bring myself to refute it because it's so very obvious I wish it were true.

I shift my weight as the clock ticks and ticks time away.

"Has he quit?"

"No," he answers but doesn't elaborate.

"Has he been fired?" I ask, and I hope not.

"Why would that happen, Miss Chambers?"

It feels like a trap, and I glance toward the closed door.

"Would you tell me the truth if I asked?" he asks me, and I don't know why I say it. Maybe I just need someone to hear it and tell me they believe me. I don't know ... but I say it anyway.

"I really loved him, and that's the truth."

"Loved?" he questions, then waves it off as if it doesn't matter. "He submitted a resignation, but I have yet to present it to the board. I don't know what to do with it."

"He resigned?" I can't believe that. "You're lying," I accuse.

"I'm not, Miss Chambers. He sent me and only me his resignation as well as a number of other interesting pieces of information."

I wait in silence.

He's taunting me and knows things I don't.

For a second, I contemplate messaging Ro to ask him what the hell is going on.

"What do you think I should do with it?" Mr. Michaels asks me.

"Burn it," I answer without thinking.

His thin lips perk up into a sad smile. "I'm not in the habit of lighting my computer on fire, young lady."

My cheeks heat with embarrassment.

"But I could certainly hit delete... although someone else may want to read it as well."

He looks at me once again like he's debating something. He's unsure of what to do, and that would make two of us.

"Have you spoken to him?" he asks.

"No," I answer, and he nods in understanding.

With a deep inhale, he says, "I didn't think you had."

"There was a lot in the email he sent me, Miss Chambers, including information about your father. In order for me to act on it, I would have to disclose everything. I'm torn on the matter."

I part my lips to say something in defense of him, but I'm left with more questions than anything else.

"I think you should speak to your fiancé," he says. I almost correct him, but I don't.

I'd be lying if I said I didn't wish he still was.

"I thought as much," he says in my silence.

"Thought what?"

"That you love him the way he loves you," he says so definitely. As if he knows when he knows nothing.

"He doesn't love me," I whisper, and I hate every word because the truth hurts more than all the lies I could scream.

"We're not together anymore," I confess.

"You should talk to him," he suggests, slipping his glasses off and folding them.

"You don't understand," I tell him.

"I understand more than you think," he says easily and glances at his watch. "I have to go now, Brooklynn. I wish you well. Please speak to him before Monday. We have the weekend to decide how to handle this, and it would be helpful if Ronan was levelheaded by then."

"I'm sure the breakup isn't as bad as you think," I tell him.

"It's far more than that, and I shouldn't be the one to tell you."

"I'm not ready to talk to him," I say honestly.

I hope he can understand that much.

Ro destroyed me.

He toyed with my heart and then left it to wilt.

Johnathan doesn't say anything at all. He merely clicks on his laptop before picking up his briefcase and leaving the computer where it sits on the long table at the front of the room.

"I have to go now, and if anyone should look at my computer screen to see the email that was sent, I would have no idea. If someone were to delete it, again..." He shrugs. "Who would know? Surely not me."

"What?" I question, mostly in disbelief.

"Please be well, Miss Chambers. And if you need me, I will

be here for you. I'm so very sorry."

His condolences are hard for me to accept, so I say nothing. I watch him leave, not quite trusting him and in slight disbelief.

Did he really resign? And what else did he send?

The door clicks shut, and the clock ticks once, then twice. It doesn't make it to three by the time I move to the computer. Before I can think straight, I read it all.

"Oh my fucking God."

Those are the only words that come to mind.

CHAPTER 28

BROOKLYN

Ro gave me ten million, and I'll spend every fucking penny to see my father burn in hell. Ro's father too.

I fucking hate them. I've never hated anyone more. They have everything they could possibly ever need in the world, and they choose to spend their time and resources hurting others. Fuck them. Fuck them straight to hell.

I always knew my family was fucked up. I always knew these circles were cutthroat. But I still managed to be shocked and feel betrayed. I'm too fucking naive for this life.

I'm surprised I made it this far.

To violate me like that, for what?

A lesson?

It's always a fucking lesson. And I take it and crawl back... but not this time.

I've had a week to process. A scream session with a therapist. And I've gone through at least a dozen bottles of wine with Aspen.

This, though, this is the cherry on top.

I've lived my life with my name dragged. With every little thing I've done highlighted and scrutinized while the people closest to me got away with every little shitty thing.

This is my wall. Videotaping a private moment and sharing it to shame me. That is something I won't let go. I don't care what it costs. I don't care what it says about me. I care about putting the truth out there for all to see.

My father will pay for what he did to me.

As if summoning the devil himself, the door to the conference room opens. He walks in first, a dark blue suit and a slim navy tie that doesn't quite match. The frown that mars his face only makes him look older.

In fact, I've never seen him look so weathered. Good.

My lawyer stands from his seat to the left of me, but I stay seated and silent.

His lawyer follows him in. A skinny fellow who looks like he's lost a few nights of sleep. Hopefully over representing this piece of shit.

My father looks at me like I'm a gnat he can't quite swat, and I hold his gaze. Inside, I'm fuming, but outside,

I feel nothing.

He's nothing to me.

Never again will he have any piece of me or part in my life.

"Please have a seat," my lawyer, Mr. Anderson, says, gesturing to the seats opposite me.

His lawyer pulls out the two chairs at once, one for him and one for my father, but my father remains standing. Just seeing him builds a rage inside me that's barely tempered, but also pain. Undeniable pain. I can't help it. I wish I could just turn it off, but I can't.

"I'm not here to fucking negotiate."

The shock on his lawyer's face mirrors my own. I can only imagine what they expected him to do versus what he intended.

He's gotten away with doing what he pleases his entire life, in business and even worse in his personal world.

"The audacity of this bitch to sue me," he sneers. "You had worse coming, ungrateful bitch."

I say nothing at first even though my throat swells with emotion, and listen to his lawyer's recommendation as professionally as possible for him to leave the room.

I wonder, had I been crying, if my father would have held it in a minute longer. Just to enjoy the pain he put me through.

"If this isn't going to go anywhere—" my lawyer starts, and his lawyer responds with frantic urgency.

"I just need a moment with my client." He steps closer to

my father, but he can't do anything to contain him. He's used to telling me how it is. He's used to getting away with treating me however he'd like. He's done it all my life.

"It must be quite a surprise that there'll be a consequence this time," I remark, keeping my expression neutral. How I'm able to keep my tone even and cool, I have no idea.

He huffs a humorless laugh and then sneers, "The only one who deserves consequence is that little shit you opened your legs for. Ronan screwed me over, and I'll never—"

I speak up, finding my voice more solid than I could have ever imagined. The lawyers speak over us, mine leaning in front of me as if I might stand. I'm not moving, but I refuse to be silent while he berates me.

"I don't give a shit. You used me. You used every fucking person you could. He could screw you over ten times more, and I'd—"

"You have no allegiance to anyone but yourself. You deserved to be punished for spreading your legs to a fucking Wolf. Selfish just like your whore of a mother. I never deserved to be stuck with a child like you."

At that comment, I stand, the legs of the chair screeching across the floor as I do. "You expect pity? After what you did? Fuck you."

Our lawyers attempt to silence us, to dispel the conversation as we stand across from each other. I hate that I gave him any emotion at all. But at least I can live knowing

I've said my piece.

"Enough!" my lawyer finally screams, and the room goes silent apart from heavy breathing. "I think it's best you and your client leave."

"Fuck you," my father snarls, and to my surprise, he tells his own lawyer off as well.

My father shoves his lawyer as he attempts to guide my prick of a parent out of the room. The door opens, and he's almost gone, almost out of my life.

Before he can leave, I tell him, "You're right about one thing..."

My father turns around to look me dead in my eyes.

"You never did deserve me."

With one last glare, the door closes, and I pray it's the last time I have to see him. I never want to even think of his face again.

I swallow thickly and grab the glass of water in front of me, eagerly drinking it and attempting to calm my racing heart.

"I apologize, Miss Chambers. I was assured your father wanted to end this suit before it began. Had I known—"

I stop Anderson and end his misery. "You don't know him like I do." I set the glass down as calmly as I can. "You couldn't have known, and I don't care either way."

"Still, I should have taken—" He attempts another apology, but that's not what I want in the least.

"I want to press every charge and file every suit," I tell him with finality. The second I discovered what happened, I demanded it. Apparently, there are steps in place. You can't simply hit a button and have to try to be "civil" first. But there's no civility in the life my father leads.

The legs of the chair beside me drag on the floor with a groan, and my lawyer takes the seat and adjusts his tie.

"Miss Chambers... may I?"

"Of course," I answer, taken aback and unsure where this conversation is going.

"Have you discussed your decision with Mr. Wolf? Ronan, I, um... to be clear. Not the other defendant in your case."

My throat goes tight with emotion. The first disturbance to what I've been feeling all day. A raw ache that reminds me of a different kind of pain. "I have not."

"It may be best," he suggests quietly.

I don't know how to tell him that I don't think I can. Especially when I know I'll have to. In order to proceed, I'll have to see him. We're two broken people brought into this world with more than we deserved, yet at the same time, lacking the one thing that mattered.

It all feels like it's just too late. Once you're aware of how deeply damaged you are, there's just no way to fix that. Especially not with the person who showed you so clearly that they saw you and they were willing to let you go.

Tears prick at the back of my eyes, and I hate how much it

hurts. My lawyer hands me a tissue, and I accept, attempting to prevent the tears from falling.

"The sooner, the better," he tells me quietly. "I believe you'll need to unblock his number," he adds, and when I look at him, he cocks a knowing brow.

So he can see, I unblock his number in front of him.

"Good. I'm in touch with his lawyers as well," he confides in me, as if him being aware that I blocked Ro's number wasn't evidence of that.

"I could tell," I answer wrly.

"I apologize again for today. I was hoping we could end this before it began."

I only nod, unable to say anything as the past months play back in my mind and torture me further. I gather my purse and coat, and walk mindlessly to my car with my lawyer by my side to ensure no other disturbances.

All the while, I watch myself fall in love in my memories.

Kissing Ro started all of this. And I know I shouldn't have done it. It set a series of events into motion that can never be undone. Moments that have changed my life forever. I don't know what will become of me—or of us—but as I sit in the front seat of my car, all of the emotions storm within me.

The most prominent is unworthiness.

How can I possibly talk to him?

How can I look him in the eye and hold his gaze?

"I can't do this," I whisper to myself, and a text comes

through.

There is a flood of messages before it.

Ronan: *I'm sorry. But I'll do everything I can to fix it.*

Fix it... What exactly is it? Does he mean us? The video? The lawsuits?

There is so much that needs to be fixed. Just a moment ago, I would have admitted to being damaged beyond repair. I've probably been that way for the better part of a decade.

I reread his text again and again.

Each time wishing I had any hope left to cling to.

CHAPTER 29

RONAN

I never expected to open my front door and see her standing there like a fucking goddess. Despite that, she immediately starts screaming at me.

"I loved you, and you lied to me!"

Those are the first words that shoot out of her as if she's spitting fire at me.

"Kitten…" I coax with my hands out in front of me in a surrendering gesture. "Did you—"

"No." She points a menacing finger at me. I keep my hands up and my mouth closed. "I didn't want to yell. I didn't want to say a word to you." She stares up at me, her doe eyes riddled with pain. My Brooklyn.

I've never felt like this before. Like I'm clinging to a single thread and so very terrified of it breaking.

"Say something," she commands.

"Did you say you loved me?" I ask.

She folds her arms over her chest in defiance, still heaving as she catches her breath. Her wide eyes stare back at me like a wounded animal. Fuck, it cuts me to see her like this, but she's here.

Yell at me. Hit me even. I don't give a shit as long as she lets me kiss her again. She noticeably swallows and ignores my question.

"How could you let me go?" she accuses, shaking her pretty little head at me. "How could you?"

"I tried to stop you."

"No! You were willing to let me be a fucking secret!"

It's then she hears Mr. Michaels and the rest of the lawyers. Their voices billow out to the foyer from where they are in the living room.

Leaning in the doorway to glance, she turns her gaze back to me and asks, "Who the hell is that?"

"I was in a meeting."

She turns to leave, but I reach out to grab her wrist.

"Stay please," I beg her as she turns and only stares at where my fingers are wrapped around her wrist. Her short red dress clings to her curves and the color matches her lips. "You look beautiful," I add and she scoffs, but she doesn't pull out of my touch. She doesn't leave.

"I want you to stay. I want you. I need you, Brooklyn."

Her bottom lip drops just slightly as she looks back at me. Almost like disbelief.

"I only came because my lawyer said I should talk to you."

"Ronan?" one of my lawyers calls out, and I ignore him, caught in her gaze.

She whispers as the footsteps approach, "I hate that I still have feelings for you."

"I hate that you hate it."

To my right, Mr. Walker comes into view. He's about my height and fit for his age. His cologne drifts toward us.

"Miss Chambers." He sounds surprised and glances at me. I can barely look back at him when she looks at me like that. Like she hates me. She has every right to.

"I think we should leave you two alone," Mr. Walker says in an exhale. He says he'll be in touch shortly and to update him if anything new needs to be addressed.

Thankfully, Brooklyn enters when he gestures her in. One step in the right direction.

The lawyers don't hesitate to stand and exit, leaving me alone with the woman I love desperately who just admitted that she loved me for one moment in time too.

BROOKLYN

In his living room, a living room we once shared, I see all the memories of us staring right back at us as if it's happening right then. I have no control over them, and I feel like I'm losing my mind with each passing second between us. I turn to face him, to tell him off once again, but the words crumble before they're spoken. My Ronan looks like a shell of himself. His hair a mess, his eyes with dark circles like he hasn't slept. And with an expression I've never seen before. Pure pain and regret echo in his gaze.

Before I can express another word, Ronan declares, "I'm a prick, a liar, and a piece of shit, but Brook, I want you. I want you more than anything I've ever wanted." His words are rushed as he stands only a few feet from me with my back to the back of the sofa.

"You want—"

"I love you, and I loved you even when I said goodbye because I wanted to protect you and—" I cross my arms again and look away, refusing to believe that he could love me and let me leave, but he reaches out to me, his hands on my forearms, and looks me in the eyes. "I regret ever dragging you into this. I blame myself, and I'm sorry. I wanted to end it because I couldn't see you like that, but I made it worse. For me and for you, and I love you. I'm sorry."

When he says it... when he says I love you, it takes a

moment to sink in. To really sink in.

"I want you in ways I never thought were possible for a man like me. I want you in all the ways I should and all the ways I shouldn't. I want you then, now, forever. It's me and you, kitten."

I don't answer him for a few seconds because I truly don't know how to take his words. Shock overwhelms me. I've never heard this man say he's sorry for anything in his life. Men like him don't apologize. However, I do know how I feel, and that's more powerful than anything I've ever experienced.

I want everything he's saying.

But mostly, I want to believe what he's confessing to me.

Instead of sharing everything my overly wrecked mind is thinking, I ask, "You want me how? To pay me—"

"I gave you more than enough for you to never need anyone, but I can give you more if that's what you want. I will do anything."

"Did they say getting back with me would let you save your job?" The snide hesitation in my tone is evident, and I don't try to hide it.

In a harsh tone, he adamantly informs, "No. They said it would be horrible press if I did."

Tears leak from my eyes, and I brush them away. I'm evidently upset and swallow thickly, feeling sick to my stomach, but I push through the emotions that have taken hold of me.

His response to my anxiety is to caress the side of my face with the back of his fingers, and I lean into his embrace because again, I have no control over my actions. It all feels too much at that moment. Fuck, I miss him. I feel myself falling all over again.

I also embrace it. Loving his hands on me in any way.

"I told him I didn't fucking care, and if they went through with any of it, I would sue just for the fucking bad press on their end. My father's been served a C&D, and he knows better than to fuck with me. He used what he had on me and has nothing left."

Lies or truths?

He continues, "I'll keep my job. But right now, it's not what I want."

Unable to help myself, I blurt, "What do you want?" I hate the hope that I cling to when I ask him that question.

All in one breath, he replies, "You. I fucked up, and I'm sorry." He looks deep into my eyes, almost like he is staring into my soul, before he confesses in private for the first time, "I love you, Brook. I've always loved you."

I resist, and he gives me the phone, showing me something on the screen.

Pointing at what appears to be a star, he states, "That one right there is yours. When it gets darker, you can see it." He points at the window.

Shocked and dismayed, I whisper, "You bought me a star?"

as if I'm asking a question.

"I named it after you."

"I—"

"Just hold that thought." He practically runs out of the room, quickly returning from the bedroom with a bright teal Tiffany bag. "I got these for you too," he says, sounding out of breath. The small bag dangles from his hand, and I stare at him with disbelief.

"Please," he presses, holding it closer to me, "It's yours."

I open it, and it's a star with our initials for all to see. It's dainty and a beautiful silver. I run my thumb over the engraving. It's breathtaking. B&R. My eyes instantly glaze, and I hold back the tears from sliding down the sides of my face.

"I wanted to buy you a constellation, but they said they don't allow that." He watches me, waiting for a reaction. "So a star in the sky and one for you to wear." He swallows, and the cords in his neck tighten. He brushes his palms on his suit pants in the silence. His black tie is loose around his neck and his collar unbuttoned. I can't deny the pull to him. The attraction. And how genuine he seems. I just don't know that I can trust him. He already broke my heart once, and I don't know what will happen to me when he inevitably does it again.

"Are you trying to buy me back?"

He shakes his head. "I know I can't do that. I know no amount of money takes back what I did, but I need you to know and understand that letting you go when you really needed me... I wish I could just go back. The moment I did it, I regretted it. I swear to you. There hasn't been a second in the day that I haven't thought about you and the very second I did what I was told to."

"Told to?" I'm visibly upset.

"My father. I didn't..." He looks away for a moment, then back at me. "I didn't do it because he told me to. I did it because if I didn't listen to him, I knew he could hurt you even worse than you were already hurting, and I knew it was all my fault, and I didn't know how to stop it any other way. I'm sorry. I'm sorry I ever did this to you. I wish I could just take it all back." Another tear slips down my cheek, and I brush it away, still unsure what to say. In my silence, he adds, "Our fathers can have each other." He huffs a laugh. "It's what they deserve."

I can't argue with him there. They do deserve every shitty, fucked-up thing coming their way.

Sensing my hesitation, he reaffirms, "What else can I do, Brook?"

"See..." I reply. "That's the part that sucks. I love you so much that I want to just say yes."

He steps toward me and grabs my chin, angling it to him. "Then do it. Say yes. But wait."

It all happens so fast, yet it still seems to play out in slow motion. He drops to one knee and pulls a ring from his pocket, showing it to me.

I open my mouth to speak, but he quickly cuts me off.

He speaks with conviction, "Marry me, Brook. For real this time." He looks up at me and I can barely believe it's happening.

"It's my mother's ring, Brook. That's how you know I mean it."

"Ro," I breathe before covering my mouth with my hand.

"I love you. I made a mistake, but I will never do it again. I can't lose you again. Marry me. Say yes. Marry me."

My body can't hold me up, and I crumple to the floor in front of him.

I can't believe what just happened. Never did I think I'd feel this way for him again, let alone stronger. Throwing all the pain he caused out the window, I decide to do what feels right for me.

For him.

For us.

Finally, I follow my heart and confirm, "Yes. I love you, Ro. I've always loved you too—"

Before the last word flies out of my mouth, he slams his lips against mine and kisses me with a force I don't expect.

"Ronan..." I rasp into his mouth. "I love you. I can't stop loving you, dreaming about you, wanting a future with you..."

He growls, slipping his tongue past the seal of my lips. I deepen his kiss, desperate for his love. How I needed this. His touch, his affection, his love.

"I love you," he breathes out against my mouth. "I love having you in my life."

"I love you," I confess back, and I know it's true.

"I'm sorry, kitten. I'm so fucking sorry. Do you hear me?"

"Ronan…"

"I've always wanted you. You're all I've ever wanted. Just you. Nobody else but you."

He doesn't let up and continues caressing me, kissing me, whispering to me that he's sorry. So fucking sorry. We walk as we kiss, and he leads me to the bedroom. I know exactly what's going to happen, and I need it. I need him. I need everything to be back to just the two of us.

"I love you, Brooklyn. I fucking love you."

Going full speed, I kiss him deeper as he pulls me against his torso. I wrap my legs around his waist before he settles me onto the bed to stand between my legs.

He pins me in front of him, locking my body with his.

We are suddenly panting profusely, overwhelmed by our emotions.

"I'm not asking you to forget what I did to your perfect heart. I'm just begging you to forgive me, and I'll spend the rest of our life together proving how sorry I am for breaking your heart. I love you, kitten. You're my whole world."

I exhale, feeling emotions I can't begin to place. Gliding my tongue into his mouth, I surrender to his passionate embrace. He can feel my chest rising and falling against his torso, my hard nipples firmly pressing against his clothed chest. He hasn't even touched me yet, and I'm already splitting at the seams for him.

"Ronan..." I express, strangled and frantic.

He kisses me until my body undeniably yields to him.

Until I'm anxious and trembling, soft and supple in his arms.

Until every muscle pulses with anticipation.

With need.

With want.

With desire to once again be his and only his.

He's my undoing.

Ronan Wolf has always been my soul mate.

Our lips move like they're made for one another. Full of desperation and urgency, desire and hunger, fighting our past and demons and our way back to each other. I can hear the pounding of his heartbeat and feel the thrumming of his pulse quickening with a rhythmic, alluring sound that both soothes and controls me in ways I never want to stop. Not for one second.

It's maddening.

Controlling.

Everything I crave it to be.

His lips move from mine, descending down my neck— pecking, nipping, licking. My head extends back even though I whimper at the loss of his mouth against mine.

It's slow and instinctual.

Further surrendering to his touch, to his love, to the man who owns my heart and soul.

"Ro... please kiss me again."

He eyes me with a predatory regard. "I will." He grins. "But first, I'm going to kiss your pussy."

Roughly gripping my thighs, he slides my ass down to the edge of the bed where he tears off my panties and dress next. Once I'm naked, he drops to the floor and sucks my clit into his mouth. My head falls back, and my back arches from the intense pleasure.

I gasp a heady breath, turned on but also startled by his aggressive gesture. He takes his time with me. Just the way I love. Inch by inch, leaving me breathless beneath him, working me into a frenzy.

Kissing.

Licking.

Fucking me with his skilled tongue.

"Beg me, kitten. Beg me to make you come."

I sit up on my elbows and plead, "Please..." He causes my back to arch when he does exactly what I ask.

I explode, coming so hard that I'm lightheaded.

"Ronan..." I purr his name, fisting my hand in his hair.

"Whose pussy is this, Brooklyn? Who owns every last part of you?"

I moan in response.

"Tell me? Tell me who you fucking belong to?" he

demands, standing above my body.

I watch as he throws off his shirt and unbuttons his slacks, pulling out his huge, hard cock.

He gives me a devious smile, looking utterly delicious. "Now answer my question."

Placing his shaft along my opening, he coats the tip with my wetness and parts my lips. Slowly and deliberately swaying up and down, he knows my clit's still sensitive from his relentless tongue.

"You," I say.

In one hard thrust, he's deep inside me. My nails dig into the comforter as the mix of pain and pleasure races through my entire body and lights every nerve ending on fire.

"Fuck me," he growls.

My hands fist the comforter in knots while he slams in and out of me.

With each moan that escapes my lips.

With each deep thrust of his cock.

With each clench of my pussy, stirring down to his balls.

I lose myself to him.

Coming.

Spasming.

Trembling.

My legs wrap around his hips, and my heels press into his ass.

He leans forward, resting his forehead on mine and

staring deep into my hooded eyes.

Our hearts pound.

Our skin's covered in sweat.

Our lungs are completely out of breath.

He makes love to me.

In our own world.

In our own everything.

All I can hear is desire over the waves crashing onto the boat, mimicking the rhythm of our hearts as he takes what belongs to him.

Me.

When he moves his hands to my clit, my breathing escalates.

"Fuck, Brook," he groans my name. "Just like that ... give it to me..."

I can feel his thickness as my orgasm hits me again. My body shivers. It's all too much, but I can't get enough.

He kisses me more aggressively than before and grabs the back of my neck, wanting to bring me closer to him. Our lips move of their own accord. We no longer have any control over our actions.

He kisses my jawline to my neck, then deliberately makes his way back up to my mouth.

"Goddamn ... you feel so fucking good," he groans, roughly gripping my hips.

Moving harder, faster, for his pleasure and mine. He can feel my G-spot on the tip of his cock, only fueling his thrusts.

My body is on the verge of shuddering as I take his vigorous assault.

Our mouths part, breathless, riding the high and waiting to fall over the edge.

Together.

He plunges his tongue into my mouth when he feels my pussy throb against his cock, pulsating long and tight. Muffling my screams.

I'm his undoing.

Another groan escapes from deep within his chest as he cums so hard and deep inside me. He releases his cum as deep into my pussy as he possibly can.

Both of us try to catch our breaths.

Our thoughts.

Our emotions.

Until he whispers at the shell of my ear, "I love you, Mrs. Wolf."

He makes me feel...

Whole again.

CHAPTER 30

BROOKLYN

"I love you." He smiles with his eyes as we celebrate our fathers having mug shots taken and my own resigning from his position at the university. It was a forced resignation and long overdue.

It's been a long three months, but it was worth it.

Before I know it, I'm stepping into a brand-new Mercedes luxury convertible. A gift from Ronan.

"You love it?" he asks me as he slips into the passenger seat.

"Uh, yeah," I answer, loving how the leather slips under my palms. "I love it, and I love you."

He's distracted me these past few months with gifts and plans for our big night and our honeymoon.

Our wedding is right around the corner.

With the key in my hand and Ronan beside me, with a devilsh smile, I can't wait to officially be Mrs. Wolf. I've never felt this kind of joy and happiness, and … freedom. It feels liberating to be done with what was, and to know whatever is to come is in my control, and it'll come with a happily ever after. We have our whole future to look forward to. And that's all I really want. That's the only gift I need: a life beside this man.

The adrenaline pumping wildly through my veins is a feeling I never forget. I feel every roar of the car as my foot eases down on the clutch. Popping the shifter into reverse, I back out of his garage.

"Holy shit!" I exclaim. "This is amazing!" The more I drive, the further my heart fucking soars, being with the man I love.

I quickly shift into second, then third, tearing down the street and gun it onto the highway. I watch in astonishment as I downshift to first, fishtailing out onto an old, abandoned road. The only sounds that can be heard are the squealing tires.

It's such a thrill.

I'm hot, burning up as my heart races.

A part of it is from the engine, and the other is from Ronan. The rush surges through my veins.

The next thing I know, he orders, "Spread your legs for me, my little whore."

"What?"

When I don't move fast enough, he does it for me. Reaching over, he slides his hand between my thighs.

"I'm going to do two of my favorite things at once, watch you drive this sports car and make you come."

Halting all the air in my lungs, I suck in a breath as soon as he starts rubbing my clit. I downshift, jerking the wheel to make a sharp right turn. The car slides, and my head falls back as his skillful fingers continue to work me over.

The engine hums as I shift into a lower gear, and he slides his finger inside me at the same time. The adrenaline coursing through me releases endorphins, skyrocketing my entire body and bringing me to a new high.

It takes over all my senses and my entire being. My chest heaves, and I try to catch my breath.

"Oh God…" I pant as he hits my G-spot over and over again.

I pull over on the vacant road in an instant, letting my head fall back as my legs tremble.

"Let's see what this baby can do," Ronan rasps, and I don't know if he's referring to me or the car, but right now, we're both trembling.

"Professor Wolf…"

Harder and harder, he fucks me with his hand. Waves of ecstasy barricade my mind as arousal slips between my legs. Our heated emotions run wild, fueling my need to come.

I'm a ticking time bomb, counting down until I explode as my eyes close and my head falls back against the fresh leather.

The groan from Ronan is the sexiest thing I've ever heard. Taking everything along with it, like a tornado spinning around in circles. It elicits feelings I never thought possible.

I feel every loss of breath.

Every curve of his finger.

It clutters my mind, and I can't keep up with his skilled assault.

"Come for me, Brook."

That's all it takes for me to fucking ignite. I shatter, coming apart at the seams. I come so hard that my vision blurs, and my body shakes uncontrollably.

Before I can say a word, he throws his seat back, grips my waist, and pulls me onto his lap. His cock is out and inside me before I can even blink.

"Ride my cock, kitten."

I don't have to be told twice. I do as I'm told—eager and desperate to give him pleasure like he gives me. He grips my hips and moves me harder against him. Pushing my pleasure higher and higher.

"Come on my cock, like you just came on my hand."

Once again, I explode, seeing fucking stars.

Galaxies.

A lunar eclipse.

He doesn't hold back when he finds his own release. He kisses down my collar, whispering between kisses, "I love you, I love you, I love you."

And I relish in the words that mean everything to me because I finally have...

Mr. Wolf.

About the Author
Willow Winters

Thank you so much for reading my romances. I'm just a stay at home Mom and an avid reader turned Author and I couldn't be happier.

I hope you love my books as much as I do!

More by Willow Winters
www.willowwinterswrites.com/books

About the Author
M. Robinson

M. Robinson is the Wall Street Journal and USA Today Bestselling author of more than thirty novels in Contemporary Romance and Romantic Suspense. Crowned the "Queen of Angst" by her loyal readers, you'll feel the cut of her pen slicing through your heart as your soul bleeds upon the words of her stories with each turn of the page. M. lives the boat life along the Gulf Coast of Florida with her two puppies and real life book boyfriend, the inspiration for all her filthy talking alphas, Bossman.

When she isn't in the cave writing her next epic love story, you can usually spot her mad-dashing through Target or in the drive-thru of Starbucks, refueling. Yes, she's a self-proclaimed shopaholic, but only if she's spending Bossman's money.

You can follow M, Ted, Marley, and Bossman on Facebook, Instagram, and her absolute favorite social platform-TikTok.

www.authormrobinson.com

This is the Discreet Edition so no-one knows what
you are reading.

You can find each edition at

www.willowwinterswrites.com/books

www.ingramcontent.com/pod-product-compliance
Lightning Source LLC
Chambersburg PA
CBHW022125310726

48972CB00007B/2195